INVASION!
"WE HAVE NO TIME
FOR DISCUSSION."

Admiral Kirschbaum continued: "A sensor array at the Furies Point has been attacked by five ships of unknown origin. I'm ordering all available ships to the area at top speed."

Captain Jean-Luc Picard's hand tightened on his empty glass mug. He set it down before it could shatter in his grip. "We're on our way, Admiral."

"Good." The admiral's mouth tightened. "I hope I don't have to explain—"

"I understand the urgency, Admiral."

"Captain Picard," Admiral Kirschbaum said heavily, "if those ships are what we believe them to be, then we're at war."

Look for STAR TREK Fiction from Pocket Books

Star Trek: The Original Series

Star Trek: The Next Generation

Star Trek: Deep Space Nine

Star Trek: Voyager

STAR TREK
THE NEXT GENERATION®

INVASION!

BOOK
TWO

THE SOLDIERS
OF FEAR

DEAN WESLEY SMITH AND
KRISTINE KATHRYN RUSCH

INVASION! concept by John J. Ordover and Diane Carey

POCKET BOOKS
New York   London   Toronto   Sydney   Tokyo   Singapore

An *Original* Publication of POCKET BOOKS

POCKET BOOKS, a division of Simon & Schuster Inc.
1230 Avenue of the Americas, New York, NY 10020

A VIACOM COMPANY

This book is published by Pocket Books, a division of
Simon & Schuster Inc., under exclusive license from
Paramount Pictures.

ISBN: 0-671-54174-9

First Pocket Books printing July 1996

10 9 8 7 6 5 4 3 2 1

POCKET and colophon are registered trademarks of
Simon & Schuster Inc.

Printed in the U.S.A.

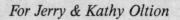

For Jerry & Kathy Oltion

THE SOLDIERS
OF FEAR

Chapter One

Lieutenant Robert C. Young, Bobby to everyone who knew him, sat with his feet on the lip of the console before him. He had the stout build of an athlete and blond hair that sometimes got a little longer than Starfleet regulation allowed. He had modified the regulation chair so that it tilted backward easily, comfort being his highest priority. Life on Brundage Station was dull, routine, and his punishment for telling Admiral Kirschbaum that nothing in Starfleet compared with snow skiing down Exhibition in Sun Valley, Idaho. On Earth.

Bobby hadn't realized he was talking with an admiral at the time, only some pompous fool who seemed to believe that every officer aspired to interstellar travel. Bobby had gone to Starfleet Academy at the urgings of his mother, a dear woman who was afraid that Bobby would spend his entire life on the slopes of the sector's snow-covered mountains and therefore never achieve anything of importance. She was afraid he would die broke and without skills; he, on the other hand, believed skiing was skill enough for any man and more than enough to live a full life.

But he loved his mother. He had joined. And because he had been a good cadet who had done well in officer training, he had gone to one too many off-campus parties, and insulted the wrong admiral.

Friends later told him that if he had made the same comment to Admiral Zlitch, she would have laughed, agreed, and then compared the latest in ski-boot technology with him.

Admiral Kirschbaum had merely said, *If you find all of the galaxy boring, young man, I have the assignment for you.*

Brundage Station, armpit of the galaxy. Some wag—another skier, obviously—fifty years before had given the station the Brundage nickname after a famous ski hill in McCall, Idaho, because, rumor had it, Brundage stood on the slippery slope to nowhere.

Brundage was now officially known as Brundage Point Listening Station. Sometimes, in the oldest references to the station, it was called the Furies Point Defensive Listening Station. Over eighty years before, some incredibly powerful beings had come through a point in space near the post, and had eventually declared themselves the enemy. In coming they had destroyed an entire solar system, the remains of which now swirled slowly in the screens. Bobby had seen the old holos, read the old materials, and studied

2

everything he could about the battle that had taken place deep in Klingon space, not because he was interested, but because it was required.

Starfleet believed the Furies would come again.

They hadn't, of course.

Other lieutenants had run Brundage Station, shifting to real duty after three years of service, always swearing they would never watch an empty part of space again.

Bobby had been here two years. After three days, he had been ready to write the admiral an apology. Now he understood what the wily old man had been about. The admiral had given Bobby easy duty to show him that truly active duty was better than sitting on his duff all day, guarding the site where a supposed enemy had appeared the year his grandfather was born.

In most ways, the duty was like any other. The station was small, and sometimes ships stopped. Bobby commanded a team of three others. In addition to the Furies Point, they monitored forty unmanned listening posts, most along the Klingon border. Occasionally they saw something. Usually they didn't.

His evening watch promised to be no different.

He had holographic brochures of several nearby ski resorts in his room, including a low-grav, highly specialized ski center on Regal III. He planned to go through all of them before he slept tonight. His first extended vacation was coming up, and he planned to enjoy every minute of it.

The observation room always seemed big to him, even though it was the size of a shuttlecraft's piloting area. The two viewscreens, opened to the vastness of space, gave an illusion of size. So did the constant emptiness and the inactivity on the control board.

He had some diagnostics to run through, but they could wait. His evening shift had a routine that kept him awake and functioning through the long, lonely hours.

A red light flashed on the control board. The light intermittently illuminated the sole on his black regulation boot. He frowned, sighed, and sat forward.

A malfunction.

At least it would give him something to do.

But the light flashing wasn't the one he expected to see.

Something had triggered the warning devices at one of the listening posts.

His hands shook with excitement, and he had to remind himself that the last time this happened, it had been caused by space debris in the listening post's delicate trigger mechanism.

His fingers flew over the console as he ran a quick systems check.

Everything was in order at both the station and the outpost. But there seemed to be a slight drop in the mass of the outpost. That made no sense at all. How could the mass of an outpost drop?

He tapped his comm badge. "Wong! Airborne! Judy! I got something happening up here."

"On our way," Wong's clear voice came through the comm. "Run the diagnostics."

"Already done," he snapped back. Wong had no right giving orders, even if he was the only one with engineering experience.

But for good measure, Bobby ran a second level of diagnostics. No sense making a mistake when he had time. It would take the others a few moments to get to the control room. They had been in their quarters. Bobby always took the graveyard shift, never liking the concept of artificial night or artificial day.

The second diagnostics checked as well. The mass of the listening post continued to drop slightly, even though that seemed impossible. Something was clearly going on out there. Just what was the question.

He let the air whistle through his teeth. Behind him the door hissed open and Wong, a slender man twice Bobby's age, hurried in.

Wong grabbed the empty chair beside Bobby's, leaned over the console, and ran a third set of diagnostics, his fingers flying over the board almost faster than the eye could follow.

"Mine already checked out," Bobby said. "Both times."

"Hmm," Wong said, apparently unimpressed. When the diagnostic finished, he said, "That makes no sense," and began a series of other tests that Bobby had only heard about. Bobby didn't stop him; better to be careful. Bobby's mouth was dry. He had never thought about what he would do if something real triggered one of the outpost alarms.

Judy hurried in next. Her long silver hair was still down, and she wore a robe over her nonregulation lounging clothes. She was tiny, in her mid-fifties, and the unofficial leader of the group. She had two fully grown children, both in Starfleet, and she liked to cook. Sometimes they even called her "Mom" and she never objected.

"What have we got?" she asked, sliding into the chair to Bobby's left.

"Something triggered one of the posts."

Wong grunted, and started yet another set of diagnostics.

"Have you run tests?"

Bobby glared at her. Did everyone think he was incompetent? "Twice," he told her.

"Hmmm," she said, as unimpressed as Wong had been.

Then Airborne burst in the door, his hair sticking up at all angles. He, like Bobby, had a tendency toward wildness. Airborne liked to jump—out of anything moving, safe or not. His tall, lanky frame had survived more broken bones than Bobby could imagine. Over the past year Bobby had been convincing Airborne that jumping off things while on skis was more fun than anything he'd tried. But Airborne had been reluctant to put in all the time learning how to ski, just to jump off rocks. He said he could do that without skis.

"More space junk in the listening posts?" Airborne asked, rubbing a hand over his sleep-puffy face.

"No," Wong said curtly. "I'm reading a major drop in mass. There's something really strange happening out there."

His tone took the levity out of the room. Bobby forced himself to swallow.

"It's for real, then," he said. He leaned forward.

"I'll get Starfleet Command," Judy said, sliding her chair toward the communications console.

"Yeah," Wong said.

Airborne came up behind him, and placed both

hands on the back of the chair. "Tell us now, Wong. No sense grandstanding."

"He's not," Bobby said. Wong never tried to take advantage of the others. He just usually thought the others were incompetent.

"Something has just destroyed the warning device at Point 473," Wong said.

Judy paused in midpunch, her hand extended over the console. "Destroyed?"

Bobby ignored her. He was pulling all the information he could on the point. "Information on 473 coming up on screen," he said.

"We don't need it," Airborne said, sinking into the only remaining chair.

Bobby glanced at him. Airborne's normally dark skin had turned a sickly shade of gray.

"The Furies Point," Wong said, his voice sounding to Bobby as if he were going to be suddenly sick.

"No," Bobby said. Sure, they'd all been prepped on the Furies battle, that was a condition of serving at the post, but the Furies tale sounded like one of those grandiose stories skiers told when they got off the hill, trying to make a normal run seem like something special.

Judy was punching the console frantically.

Airborne was double-checking Wong's information. Airborne had a thing about the Furies. He liked to goad the others with stories of them when the tour got too routine.

"Damn," he whispered.

Bobby didn't want to know. But he had to. "Did you scan the area?"

Airborne shook his head. "Just confirmed the point

number," he said. "The listening post is gone and we got some strange things happening out there."

Before he lost complete control of the situation, Bobby had to do something. "Well, then, keep scanning it. I want to know exactly what's going on."

"I don't," Airborne whispered. But he bent over the console just the same.

His fingers flew over the console.

"You got Starfleet yet?" Bobby asked Judy.

"No, sir," she said, automatically slipping into protocol. Bless her.

Wong let out a breath. "There seems to be a very large temporal disturbance," he said, "almost as if a black hole has formed where the beacon used to be. Only it's much more than a black hole. More like a tear in space."

"Oh, man," Airborne said. He was hunched over his console. "Bobby—ah, Lieutenant, sir—I've got a reading near there of five ships. They just appeared."

"What?" Bobby hadn't seen any ships a moment before. He stopped the scrolling information, and turned the screen back toward Point 473. Even on full magnification, he still couldn't see anything.

"I've got the same thing, sir," Wong said. "There seem to be five ships surrounding the disturbance, all in stationary positions. And they're huge!"

"Can you identify the ships?" Bobby asked, making sure to keep his voice level.

Wong shook his head. Bobby scooted his chair over and looked at the readings. He'd never seen anything like them before. At least not in all the manuals he'd studied.

"Two have left position and are headed this way," Wong said.

"How long?" Bobby asked.

Wong glanced at the panel. "Three minutes."

"They've come back," Airborne said, his voice trembling. Bobby watched as Airborne seemed to shake himself, then take a deep breath.

"I've reached Starfleet, sir," Judy said.

Bobby let out breath he hadn't realized he was holding. "Scramble this message," he said.

He waited the two beats until Judy nodded that it was done; then he started. "This is Brundage Point Observation Station. We have a Priority One Emergency."

Wong and Judy both gasped, and Bobby knew why. A Priority One Emergency was the highest there was in Starfleet. But if Airborne was right, then they would need all the help they could get.

"Two minutes," Wong said. His voice was shaking.

Admiral Kirschbaum's face filled the screen. Bobby was actually relieved to see his old nemesis. "Go ahead, Lieutenant."

Bobby squared his shoulders and made himself speak with authority, not panic, even though he could feel the rising tension in the room. "The beacon at the Furies Point was destroyed. Our scans showed a small drop in mass of the beacon before it vanished. Now a large temporal disturbance has formed where the beacon used to be and five very large ships of unknown origin have taken up positions around it. Two are headed this way and will be within firing distance shortly."

Bobby watched as Admiral Kirschbaum's face went pale and he swallowed hard. "Five ships?"

Bobby nodded. "Yes, sir. Five."

Admiral Kirschbaum leaned toward the screen. "Can you evacuate before they arrive?"

Bobby glanced at Wong. He shook his head.

"There's no time, sir," Bobby said. "Those two ships are almost on us."

Kirschbaum straightened and nodded once, the closest thing Bobby would ever get to an apology. "Remember your training, Lieutenant. Anything that comes from Point 473 must be considered a Furies vessel. Consider those ships hostile, and their approach an act of war. Respond accordingly. Understand? Relay everything you are getting through this channel for as long as you can."

"Done," Judy said beside Bobby. "Starfleet is getting it all. And I've downloaded all our logs."

Bobby glanced up at the two black ships growing on the screen beside Admiral Kirschbaum's face. They were like no ships he'd ever seen, not even in the old holos of the first Furies attack. These ships were black with swept-back wings. They looked like a bird in a dive for a kill.

"An act of war," Bobby repeated. He clenched his fists. "Yes, sir."

"Good luck to you all," Kirschbaum said, and cut the picture.

The silence in the room was louder than anything Bobby had ever heard. Then Airborne put his head in his hands.

They didn't have time for despair. Bobby had to act.

10

"Get those shields up and all weapons at ready," he ordered.

"I'm still feeding all information and telemetry," Judy said.

Bobby reached into the panel below and removed the emergency phasers. He found only three. He would give them to his staff. He was the only one in uniform. He already had a phaser.

"Both ships have stopped," Wong said as Bobby laid a phaser on the panel beside him. "I can't seem to get a scan on them."

Suddenly a red beam shot from what looked like the beak of one ship.

The station's shields flared a bright blue, then red, then white. The station shook and tumbled as if riding a wave. Bobby gripped the console. "Report!" he snapped.

"Screens are down," Judy said as the firing broke off. "They seem to be hailing us."

"On screen."

Judy nodded. The screen cleared. In the second before the image appeared, Bobby felt as if a bolt of sheer terror struck him in the back of the head and shimmered down his spine. His first real command. The feeling had to be because this was his first real command moment.

He forced himself to breathe, but the air caught in his lungs as the terror filled him.

Then the blankness on the screen resolved itself into a large scarlet face, with a black snout, and ram's horns instead of ears. The eyes were long and narrow, and in the corners feeding maggots looked like tears.

Judy gasped, Airborne buried his head in his arms,

11

and Wong pushed his chair back as if the thing could come out of the screen and attack him.

Bobby's fists were clenched so hard that his nails were digging into his palm. The terror in the room seemed to shimmer and grow as if it were a real thing.

Bobby forced himself to breathe. Again he failed.

The creature on the screen opened its mouth. Silver saliva dripped from sharp, pointed teeth. "Surrender," the creature said in a voice so deep, so powerful, that Bobby could feel it in his toes. "Or be destroyed."

Then the image winked out.

Bobby didn't move. He couldn't. The sheer terror he was feeling had him frozen in place. But he had to move, for the sake of the others.

Judy and Wong were still staring at the screen, their mouths wide. Airborne raised his head. His carefree attitude was completely gone. His eyes were dark holes in his face.

"History is repeating itself," he whispered. "For the second time in a hundred years the devil has opened the gates to hell."

Bobby took two quick breaths, then said, "And for the second time we'll close it." He made his voice sound as firm and confident as he could, as he imagined a perfect Starfleet officer would do. But he didn't believe a word he said.

Chapter Two

A DROP OF SWEAT ran down Will Riker's face. He gripped the control stick of his jet firmly with both hands and pulled into a steep climb away from the bluish green ocean waters below. A stream of bright red laser fire flashed past his cockpit as the force of his climb pinned him into his seat.

He hadn't used these old atmosphere dogfight simulations since his days in the Academy, and his lack of practice was showing. He was ranked as one of the best space pilots in Starfleet and the best on the *Enterprise*, but these old dogfight holodeck simulations used ancient jets at low planet altitudes and kept score with laser hits. Twenty hits and you were considered downed.

The screen in front of him lit up bright red, indicating he'd taken a hit on his port wing. "Damn," he said softly, swinging his plane over into a tight barrel roll before the stream of laser fire could cause more damage. A full-second burst of laser fire in the center of a plane would easily count as more than twenty hits and end the game.

This time he managed to escape with only one hit.

"That's fifteen for me," his opponent, Lieutenant Sam Redbay, said through the headphones, as Redbay's plane streaked past on Riker's starboard. "You're out of shape, Will."

"Out of practice," Riker said, slamming his plane into a sharp turn in an effort to get Redbay back into his sights. "Just out of practice in these old things. Program a space dogfight and we'll see who's out of shape."

"Excuses, excuses," Redbay's voice came back. "We'll try that tomorrow."

Riker laughed as he pulled up behind Redbay's streaking jet and got him in his sights. "That's a deal."

Riker could see his old friend laughing at him right now. Redbay was a tall, thin redheaded man who moved slowly, as if the world around him was in too much of a hurry. He laughed a lot, and his freckle-faced grin was infectious to most people around him, including Riker.

The red light on the board showed he had a computer lock on Redbay's plane. "Now," Riker said, and fired, but he was an instant late. Redbay took his plane down and twisted, moving away from the stream of laser fire from Riker.

No hits. Again he'd missed. He had to admit, his old friend was good. Very good.

14

Riker shook his head and attempted to follow the other jet at the steep downward angle. At one time he and Redbay were evenly matched fighters at this holodeck simulation game. In their last year at the Academy, they had rented the holosuites and programmed dogfight after dogfight. And with each fight, not only did their skill and reflexes get better, but the stakes rose, too. It started with bragging rights, then lunches, then escalated to cleaning rooms. Their last match, the day before graduation, Riker had won and promised Redbay a rematch.

But until today, that rematch had not been possible. Now, since Redbay's assignment to the *Enterprise,* it was possible. And Riker had to admit he was enjoying this, even though he was losing badly.

"More excuses, Will?" Redbay's voice came back strong as his plane flashed past. Riker could imagine his friend's red hair and his freckled face grinning. He was probably doing everything in his power to not laugh out loud.

"All right," Riker said, laughing instead. "Excuses, then. But I won't make them for long."

Redbay's choked laugh let his enjoyment come back clearly to Riker. Then Redbay said, "Actually, Will, I wouldn't have expected you to be up on the latest atmosphere-dogfight techniques. I can't imagine how you'd have time, being first officer on a ship like *Enterprise.*"

Riker heard and understood the mixture of envy and admiration in Redbay's tone. They had been on the same career track at the Academy. Their differences were minor: Redbay had taken two more piloting points than Riker; Riker had been evaluated higher in the politics of persuasion. Their classmates had always seen a rivalry between them, but no real rivalry had actually existed, even in these made-up dogfights. They had been best of friends, and would never have gotten as far as fast without each other.

Then they separated, Redbay to years of test-piloting the latest high-speed shuttles for Starfleet, Riker to work on starships. It wasn't until a reunion several years back, when Riker had asked Redbay why he hadn't gone into starships, that Redbay leaned back, frowned, and said, *I was planning to. I just lost track of it.*

You still can, my friend, Riker had said, *but if you wait too much longer, you'll be off the career track.*

Redbay had nodded, and the next thing Riker knew, Redbay was flying his first mission on the *Starship Farragut.* His skills and deportment led to numerous promotions, until he got the plum: a berth on the Federation's flagship, the *Enterprise.*

"With you here, I'll make the time," Riker said. "You never know when it might come in handy. But tomorrow we add in space combat."

"Deal," Redbay's voice said. "But in the meantime, you might want to watch your ass."

Riker slammed his plane hard to the left as a string of red laser fire flashed past. Then, in a quick thrust, he pulled his plane up and into a tight loop. For a moment he wasn't sure if it was going to work; then Redbay's plane dropped into sight and quickly into his scope.

Computer lock. Riker fired.

Redbay moved up and left, but not before Riker caught him with a shot.

"That's ten for me," Will said.

"You were setting me up," Redbay's voice came back. This time the laughter and enjoyment were clear in his voice.

"Excuses, Sam?" Riker asked sweetly.

"You're still behind," Redbay said. "And just wait until tomorrow in a no-grav battle. I'll show you a stunt or two."

Riker laughed. "You may be famous for the Redbay Maneuver, but don't think I don't know about it. And how it's done."

Redbay laughed. "Been studying the books, huh? That's only one of many maneuvers I have up my sleeve. You don't test-pilot for Starfleet for as many years as I did and not learn a few tricks."

"I won't be as easy as you think," Riker said, laughing as he rolled his plane into a tight turn, trying to spot where Redbay had gone. But the other plane was nowhere in sight.

The his comm badge trilled.

He let go of the stick with one hand and tapped it. "Riker."

"Commander." Captain Picard's rich voice sounded strained. "I need you in my ready room. Immediately."

"Yes, sir," Riker said. "I'll be right there. Computer. End simulation."

The blue air, white clouds, and world around Riker vanished, leaving him sitting inside a sphere suspended in midair over the floor of the holodeck. Beside him was another sphere. Inside, Redbay was pulling off his helmet and undoing his seat straps. He glanced over at Riker and then back down to finish

17

the work on his straps. He looked serious. Very serious. He too had caught the captain's tone.

Redbay climbed out and dropped to the floor. He was sweating and his workout suit was sticking to him. Behind him, the sphere dissolved. "We'll have to finish this another time."

Riker grinned as he climbed out of his control sphere. "Have the computer save this game. I can still recover."

"That's what I'm afraid of," Redbay said, patting Riker on the back.

Riker nodded, then exited the holodeck, the game already forgotten.

The air in the corridor was cool, and it made him shiver despite the sweat that coated him. Everything had been fine when he left the bridge a little while ago. He wondered what could have rattled Captain Picard so quickly.

Or for that matter, what could have rattled Captain Picard at all.

The message from Starfleet had been curt. Assemble the senior officers. Prepare for a Priority One Message at 0900. Picard hadn't heard a Security One Message since the Borg were headed for Earth. The highest-level code. Extreme emergency. Override all other protocols. Abandon all previous orders.

Something serious had happened.

He leaned over the replicator. He had only a moment until the senior officers arrived.

"Earl Grey, hot," he said, and the empty space on the replicator shimmered before a clear glass mug filled with steaming tea appeared. He gripped the mug by its handle and took a sip, allowing the liquid to calm him.

He had no clue what this might be about, and that worried him. He always kept abreast of activity in the quadrant. He knew the subtlest changes in the political breeze. The Romulans had been quiet of late; the Cardassians had been cooperating with Bajor. No new ships had been sighted in any sector, and no small rebel groups were taking their rebellions into space. Maybe it was the Klingons?

He should have had an inkling.

His door hissed open and Beverly Crusher came in. Geordi La Forge was beside her, and Data followed. The doctor and Geordi looked worried. Data had his usual look of expectant curiosity.

The door hadn't even had a chance to close before Deanna Troi came in. She was in uniform, a habit she had started just recently. Worf saw her and left his post on the bridge, following her to his position in the meeting room.

Only Commander Riker was missing, and he was the one most needed. Picard couldn't access the message without him.

It was 0859.

Then the door hissed a final time and Will Riker came in. His workout clothes were sweat-streaked, his hair damp. He had a towel draped over his shoulder, which he instantly took off and wadded into a ball in his hands.

"Sorry, sir," he said, "but from your voice, I figured I wouldn't have time to change."

"You were right, Will," Picard said. "We're about to get a message from Starfleet Command. They requested all senior officers be in attendance—"

The screen on the desk snapped on with the Federation's symbol, indicating a scrambled communiqué.

"Message sent to Picard, Captain, *U.S.S. Enterprise,* and the senior members of his staff," said the generic female computer voice. "Please confirm identity and status."

Picard placed a hand on the screen on his desk. "Picard, Jean-Luc, Captain, *U.S.S. Enterprise,* Security Code 1-B58A."

When the security protocol ended, the Federation symbol disappeared from the screen, replaced by the battle-scarred face of Admiral Kirschbaum. His features had tightened in that emotionless yet urgent expression the oldest—and best—commanders had in times of emergency.

"Jean-Luc. We have no time for discussion. A sensor array at the Furies Point has been destroyed. Five ships of unknown origin are there now, along with what seems to be a small black hole. Two of the ships attacked the Brundage Station. We lost contact and don't know the outcome as yet. I'm ordering all available ships to the area at top speed."

The Furies Point. Picard needed no more explanation than that. From the serious expressions all around him, he could tell that his staff understood as well.

Picard's hand tightened on the empty glass mug. He set it down before he could shatter it with his grip. "We're on our way, Admiral."

"Good." The admiral's mouth tightened. "I hope I don't have to explain—"

"I understand the urgency, Admiral."

"If those ships are what we believe them to be, we're at war, Jean-Luc."

How quickly it happened. One moment he was on the bridge, preparing for the day's duties. The next, this.

"I will act accordingly, Admiral."

The admiral nodded. "You don't have much time, Jean-Luc. I will contact you in one hour with transmissions from the attack on the Brundage outpost. It will give you and your officers some idea of what you are facing."

"Thank you, Admiral," Picard said.

"Godspeed, Jean-Luc."

"And to you," Picard said, but by the time the words were out, the admiral's image had winked away.

Picard felt as if someone had punched him in the stomach.

The Furies.

The rest of the staff looked as stunned as he felt.

Except for Data. When Picard met his gaze, Data said quietly, "It will take us two-point-three-eight hours at warp nine to reach Brundage Station."

"Then lay in a course, Mr. Data, and engage. We don't have time to waste."

Chapter Three

THE LIGHT SEEMED TO GROW in intensity inside his eyelids as Bobby struggled to wake up. That had been one terrific nightmare. The Brundage Station attacked and overrun by the devil. Wow. He'd have to tell Judy about that.

He was hot.

He pushed at the blankets, but he was uncovered. Then he moaned. He would have to get up now and fix the environmental controls. Someone had probably messed with his room as a joke. The other members of the crew knew that Bobby Young hated temperatures above thirty-two degrees Celsius. He also hated humidity, and the faint smell of sulfur was making his nose itch.

He felt melted to the bed, as if his body made a permanent indentation in the mattress. A band tightened across his chest. Next time he would warn them; his lungs seemed to expand in the heat, and it was not a pleasant sensation. Maybe he would even order them, as their commanding officer, not to play games anymore.

The light grew in intensity, so that the protection of his eyelids felt thin and unimportant.

His bed was softer than this one, and he realized that no one could mess with his environmental controls, not since Wong had made his room a virtual sauna. After that Bobby had put three different levels of security devices on all his personal effects, including room controls.

A chill ran down his spine despite the heat. The feeling of the nightmare returned, thick and heavy.

"What in the—?" He tried to sit up, but the band on his chest turned into a restraint. He tried to grab at it with his hands, and found that his arms were imprisoned across the biceps.

He forced his eyes open. The light was blinding and he couldn't see beyond it. He had never seen a light so bright. His eyes watered, and a stabbing pain shot through his head. He tried to bring an arm up, but the restraints caught him.

He couldn't protect himself.

If this was a practical joke, it had better end quickly.

Although deep down, he knew it wasn't.

He swallowed, took a deep breath, and tried to keep the panic out of his voice. "Judy? Airborne? Wong? What's going on?"

No one answered. His shiver grew. He took a deep

breath of air that tasted of sulfur and was so humid that it burned his lungs. It hadn't been that bad a moment before. He coughed, jerking against the restraints, feeling bruises form on his chest. The heat grew more intense, and he almost thought he felt the lick of flames on his legs.

"Wong?" Bobby tried again, only this time his voice wobbled.

Laughter startled him. Deep, throaty laughter that made him want to back away, only he couldn't. He was strapped in place.

"I am afraid your friends can no longer hear you."

The voice sounded mechanical and forced. Suddenly the bright light shut off, and Bobby slowly opened his eyes. Green, red, and black spots danced in front of him. Behind the spots, he could see a figure. He squinted, and his eyes adjusted.

A face came into view.

A red, smiling face.

A face covered with maggots that crawled in and out of its long slanted eyes.

A face with a black snout.

A face with ram's horns in place of ears.

Bobby screamed.

A red hand the texture of leather covered his mouth. Long yellow fingernails scratched his skin.

The hand smelled of rotted flesh. Bobby tried to twist away, but he couldn't.

"You may scream only when I allow you to," the creature said. "I enjoy screaming—in its proper place. Now is not the time. You will be quiet, won't you?"

Bobby swallowed, trying to keep his gorge from rising.

"Won't you?"

Bobby nodded.

"Good. When I release your mouth, we will have a civil discussion." The creature's voice was deep and cultured, at odds with its appearance, and somehow more menacing because of it. This was no monster that Bobby was facing. This was something evil. Intelligent and evil. And it knew how to get at him, like some nightmare loosed by his own mind.

"Won't we?"

Bobby nodded again. The creature's breath was as foul as its skin. The creature removed its hand. Bobby's skin crawled where the creature had touched him. Despite his best efforts not to, Bobby wiped his mouth against his shoulder.

The creature laughed. Heat from its mouth touched him like tiny flames.

Bobby shuddered. He tried to hold his body still, but he had never felt such an urge to run in his entire life. The creature's mouth was full of long sharp teeth, and threads of saliva showed each time it parted its lips.

The saliva shimmered green.

"What do you want from me?" Bobby asked. He needed to gain control of this situation. If he could get the creature to tell him what it needed, maybe he could leave then.

That was the only solution he could think of. All his Starfleet training had abandoned him except for a last, tenuous grasp on the panic building within.

Somehow this thing had breached all of his internal defenses and made him feel like a frightened child again instead of an officer.

"Such an original question." The creature grinned at him, revealing those awful pointed teeth and that green-tinged saliva. Bobby tried to suppress his recoil. "Isn't it?"

"We were told we should always expect it of humans," another voice answered. A face appeared behind the creature's. An almost human face, but not quite. She had stunning features: oval eyes, a narrow nose, and high cheekbones. But Bobby barely noticed them.

His gaze was on her hair. Or what should have been her hair. Instead the strands moved on their own. It took only a moment for him to realize that he wasn't seeing hair, but small, writhing snakes that hissed and snapped at him.

Poisonous snakes.

Rattlers, cobras, copperheads.

She smiled. She knew what he was looking at. She touched the snakes almost as if trying to make sure they were in place and perfect.

"What do we want from you?" she asked as she leaned closer to him. The creature leaned with her. "Simple. We want to know your fear. You see, we like your fear. We enjoy it. And we want to use it." She laughed and the snakes surrounding her head moved even faster.

A maggot fell from the creature's eyes onto Bobby's face.

Bobby screamed, trying to shake it off. The creature

laughed as it bent over and pulled the intense bright light back over Bobby's face.

"Now," the voice said. "Tell us what we want to know. Give us all your fear."

And into the bright, intense white light, Bobby screamed again.

And again.

Chapter Four

AT 1000, PICARD'S SENIOR STAFF had reassembled in the conference room. In the last hour, Data had ingested all the historical information he could find on the Furies. Riker had prepared the crew for the possibility of war. Troi had advised families on how to protect the children from the difficulties the starship would face.

The list went on. Picard knew that each task had just begun when he needed the staff in the conference room again. La Forge had managed to get the engineering crew to double-check the engines and weaponry; Dr. Crusher had revamped sickbay into an emergency center; and Worf had prepared his security team. But none of those jobs could be finished in an hour. To prepare for battle of this scale took days, sometimes weeks.

During the last hour Picard had studied Captain Kirk's personal logs from the first *Starship Enterprise,* and the information he found unnerved him. Kirk had been called in by a panicked Klingon admiral who felt he needed one devil to fight another. As it turned out, the Klingon had been right. Kirk and the original *Enterprise* had defeated the huge Fury ship. But just one Fury ship destroyed much of a Klingon fleet before Kirk managed to win.

Picard glanced around. His officers all sat at the conference table. His seat at the head was empty, because he couldn't sit. He had to pace.

The transmission from Brundage Station had just played on the screen. Protocol had obviously been lax on Brundage—not unusual on a distant outpost—but the four station members had worked with professionalism once the crisis became apparent.

Except for the fear they had all displayed when that horrible visage appeared on their screen. Picard had understood their fear. That face, vaguely similar to the demons portrayed in European artwork and sculpture, had sent a shiver through him. But he had held that feeling back. He had seen worse things in his time.

How the crew of the Brundage station reacted bothered him at a deep level. Those reactions were not normal for trained Starfleet officers.

The view of the Furies' descent on the station, and of the subsequent attack, had left him with a restless energy—one he wouldn't have time to vent, since he knew the admiral would appear on screen at any moment.

The conference room was silent. That in itself was

unusual. His staff would normally have taken the time afforded by the delay in transmission to discuss what they had just seen.

Then the screen filled with the admiral's face. His skin was ashen, his eyes hollow points. That tape had unnerved Picard after one viewing. He didn't know how he would have felt after several.

His gaze met the admiral's, and an understanding carried across the light-years.

"Even though the ships you saw are radically different in design and shape from the first Fury ship, we have no doubt that we are facing the Furies," Admiral Kirschbaum said without preamble. "I don't need to tell you what this means."

Picard nodded. He was turned away from his staff, but he heard nothing from them.

The admiral's lips tightened. His skin seemed to have lines where it hadn't had any earlier in the day. "The *Enterprise* will be the first ship on the scene, Captain. We need information about the Furies. We need to know how many ships they have sent through the Furies Point. And if the point is a wormhole, as James T. Kirk and the first crew of the *Enterprise* suspected, then we need to know all we can about that anomaly. It seems to interact only with the Furies, which isn't like any wormhole we know."

"Either that, or they know when it will open," Picard said. "And they were waiting for it."

The admiral nodded. "The *Starships Madison* and *Idaho* are six hours away. They will arrive as quickly as they can. There are two smaller Federation ships that will join you, but they will be hours behind the starships. Don't count on them."

Three starships against five Fury ships. From what Picard had read in Kirk's logs, that would not be anywhere near enough if it came down to a fight.

"For the moment," the admiral said, "that's all we can spare. We will be setting up fallback lines of defense in case you have no success."

"I understand," Picard said. And he did understand. The *Enterprise*'s proximity to the Furies Point was the luck of the draw. It meant, though, that Picard's ship and his crew would be the first line of defense in a war that would be difficult to win.

Cannon fodder was what his ancestors called that position.

The admiral knew it too. "Captain, do your best to negotiate, discover what they want. Kirk had some success with that the first time around. His personal logs report he felt that Vergo Zennor of the Fury ship *Rath* was his friend."

"I have read Kirk's reports and logs."

The admiral nodded. "Good, but I must be clear on one point. If there's a way to close that wormhole, take it. No matter what the cost."

The chill Picard had felt on viewing that tape grew. He always knew commanding the *Enterprise* might come to this. He was willing to take those risks, but like any commander he always hoped he would never have to.

No matter what the cost.

And only three starships against all the power of the Furies.

"We will do everything we can, sir," Picard said. "The Klingons are nearby. Have they been contacted?"

The admiral grimaced. "They have, but after their first run-in with these monsters, I doubt—"

"The Klingons will fight." Worf growled the words. "I guarantee it."

"Mr. Worf," Picard said. His officers knew better than to speak out of turn.

"It's all right, Captain," Admiral Kirshbaum said. "I understand that Klingon honor is at stake here. We are counting on that. We are hoping that they will be able to overcome their memories of that first battle, and their fears. Indeed, we are hoping for help from a number of quarters. But I am afraid, Jean-Luc, that this will not change the fact that you will be on the scene first. Whatever you do will affect the future of this sector."

"I understand, Admiral," Picard said. "But there is one more matter."

The admiral nodded, as if he knew what Picard was going to say.

"Where is the Furies' lifepod containing the poppets?"

Around the room Picard could hear his staff moving, stirring, wondering just what he was talking about. But the admiral knew about the poppets from the first Fury ship. The Furies, it seemed, carried poppets, images of themselves stuffed full of pieces of their lives. Vergo Zennor had filled a lifepod with all the poppets of the crew of the first Fury ship and, right before the ship exploded, sent the lifepod into space. Kirk picked the poppets up and had them stored, waiting for just this time.

"They are being picked up from storage by the *Starship Idaho*. Use them as you see fit."

"Understood," Picard said.

"Good luck, Jean-Luc," the admiral said.

"Thank you, sir."

The admiral's image winked out.

Picard tugged on his shirt and turned to face his staff. Worf was glowering. "Captain, I apologize—"

"You were out of line, Mr. Worf," Picard said. "But the admiral understood, as did I. We may be heading into one of the most difficult battles we have ever faced."

Picard paced back and forth, talking. "One Fury ship nearly defeated the entire Klingon fleet the first time. It was only through the ingenuity of the original *Enterprise* crew that that ship was defeated. Captain Kirk's logs warn that the Furies are extremely intelligent and very powerful. He said, quite explicitly, that he believed the tactics he used eighty years ago cannot be used in any future attack. He believed that if the Furies returned, they would return stronger, smarter, and even more prepared than they had been before."

Picard took a deep breath and went on. "It is thought that complete information about our cultures and capabilities was sent back to the Furies' homeworld before their first ship, *Rath*, was destroyed. They know as much about us as we do about them."

He went on. "Federation tacticians have speculated that when or if the Furies returned, their technology would be equal to or greater than our own. We must be prepared for this. We are going against an enemy that is both cunning and advanced. We must be careful never to underestimate them."

Deanna Troi's hands were folded tightly. Geordi La Forge was toying nervously with his VISOR. Riker was tapping his fingers on the conference table. They all stared at him.

Only Data seemed calm.

"We only have another hour," Picard said. "In that time, I want you to remind your staff about the Furies' effect. The way they look can stir buried fears. Unlike the first *Enterprise,* we are prepared. The Furies may try to use our fear of them against us, but they will not succeed."

His officers stared at him, their gazes intense and focused.

"I want you all to use the files. Mr. La Forge, I want you to analyze the Kirk-Furies battle from an engineering perspective. Their first ship had the ability to use energy from weapons fired at it. I want to know how to counteract that if these new ships can do the same."

La Forge nodded.

Picard turned to Data. "Mr. Data, review the myths from every culture represented on this ship. Deanna, work with Data."

"Yes, sir," Data said. Deanna only nodded.

"Mr. Worf, you and Commander Riker will study the original battle from a tactical standpoint. No use repeating the same mistakes. And watch how the *Rath* responded. They may have a tactic we can use against them."

"Yes, sir," both Worf and Riker said at the same time.

"Very well, people," Picard said, moving over behind his chair. "Let's get to our stations. We have a great deal of work to do in a very short time."

The officers stood as a unit and filed out the door.

No conversation, no joviality, no conviviality. Only a determination to survive the next few hours.

They would need all the determination they had. If the research done since the first ship appeared was correct, the Furies had once ruled all of this sector of space. They had somehow been pushed out and only luck and Captain Kirk had kept them from returning the first time.

Now they were trying again.

As he watched his senior officers leave, he silently wished he could talk to Captain Kirk. Somehow Kirk had defeated hell itself and closed the door. Now that door had opened again. And unless it was slammed shut, the old term "hell on earth" would take on an entirely new meaning.

Or a very old one.

Chapter Five

RIKER'S BACK ITCHED. Even though he grabbed a moment to change into his uniform, he hadn't been able to shower off the sweat from his mock dogfight with Redbay since the crisis began. He felt as if he had been on the bridge for days instead of hours.

Deanna would say it was easier to concentrate on the minor discomfort than the problems ahead.

She would probably be right.

He had been on edge ever since he saw that tape from Brundage Station.

The others had too. Captain Picard was unusually silent. Worf was even more taciturn than usual. But it was Deanna that Riker worried about. As she had left the conference room, she had had a preoccupied look, as if she were concentrating on voices within instead of events without.

She and Data were working in the science officer's station, and occasionally Riker glanced over from his chair beside the captain.

"Brundage Station is within scanner range," Worf said, his deep voice booming from the security station behind Riker. "The station appears to be undamaged."

The captain sat up straighter. The news had obviously surprised him. It had surprised Riker too. From what he had seen on the transmission from the Brundage Station, the Furies attacked first. Riker assumed that when the transmission to Starfleet had been cut off, the station had been destroyed. Obviously the captain had thought the same thing.

"Put it on screen, Mr. Worf."

The captain stood and took two steps toward the screen as if he were going to have a conversation with whatever appeared. He had been filled with an odd energy that Riker had never seen before. It almost seemed as if he were nervous, his movements as out of character as Deanna's.

"Magnify," the captain said.

Riker turned his attention to the screen. Brundage Station looked normal. He had expected to see signs of the Furies' presence, but the station looked as it always had: a cylinder hanging in space. The surface of the station was covered with antennas and sensor dishes. Riker saw nothing unusual. No laser blasts. No holes.

And yet . . .

Something was wrong. He could feel it. It was a cursed place, a place where people had died, a place where evil had happened.

He forced those thoughts to the back, then glanced over his shoulder at Deanna. Her wide eyes were filled with apprehension. She felt it too—

Or was she picking up his mood? His fears. He had to control his mind and focus.

He got up abruptly and walked to Captain Picard's side.

"Captain," Data said, his voice seeming almost unreasonably calm, "the station is still functioning normally. The environmental controls are operational, the weapons systems are on-line, and the computer array seems to be intact."

"Could this be an illusion?" Riker asked.

"No, sir," Data said. He paused. "The scans also show one life-form is still aboard the station."

"A Fury?" The captain asked.

"No, sir. According to the readings, this life-form is human."

"It is a trick," Worf said. "The Havoc are doing what they can to get us aboard that station."

"Are you getting different readings, Mr. Worf?" the captain asked.

"No, sir." Worf crossed his arms over his massive chest. "It would be logical, after the attack we saw, to assume that the Havoc—what humans call the Furies—have left the station intact to lure us aboard. It is a very old trick of combat."

It seemed likely to Riker too. "Perhaps we should beam the life-form aboard the *Enterprise*," he said.

"But if we follow Mr. Worf's logic, we don't know what we're beaming aboard, do we, Number One?" The captain asked the question in a tone that required no answer. He walked up the steps to the security station. "The admiral reported five Fury ships. Where are they now?"

"The five ships of unknown design are surrounding the Furies Point, sir," Data said. "While this design of the ship matches the one seen by the Brundage Station crew, it matches nothing we have in our records, including the original Fury ship, the *Rath*. We are only assuming these are Fury ships."

"Thank you, Data." Picard nodded, and glanced at Worf's relay himself. Then he looked at the helmsman. "Mr. Filer, take us to a position between the station and those ships."

Riker felt his mouth go dry. He knew the drill. The captain was following a very clear protocol. Riker knew what the next order would be.

"Number One, take an away team onto Brundage Station. Gather as much information as you can, and find that life-form. Be prepared for anything, as Mr. Worf so clearly reminded us. We will keep a lock on you at all times. Use the emergency beam-out at the first sign of trouble."

Riker strode up the stairs toward the turbolift. "Aye, sir," he said. He could only take a handful of people. This would be a risky away mission. But he had to take people who could absorb a lot of information in a short period of time. "Data, you're with me."

Data stood from his seat at the science station, and hurried toward the turbolift. Riker tapped his comm badge. "Mr. La Forge, meet me in transporter room three."

The turbolift's doors closed around them. Riker wiped his damp palms on his pants legs. "Transporter room three," he said.

The faint reassuring whir of the lift filled the room.

"I do not understand the level of anxiety the crew seems to be feeling," Data said. "Captain Picard assured us that we would have no trouble facing the Furies as just another life-form, yet his actions seem to say otherwise. Is it a fear of how they look?"

"No," Riker said, more harshly than he intended. "We don't fear looks."

"Yet the crew seems on edge. Or am I perceiving this incorrectly?"

"Data, we've all been trained for the return of the Furies from the beginnings of our careers."

Data nodded, looking solemn. "I would think that would reduce the anxiety instead of raise it. Or am I again misinterpreting the response?"

"It's a little more complicated than that, Data," Riker said, and stopped as the lift's doors opened onto the transporter room. Anderson, the transporter chief, was already in position, hands on the controls.

"The captain says I'm to monitor your every movement," Anderson said.

"See that you do," Riker said.

Data shot him a puzzled look.

Riker realized he *was* on edge. He usually had more finesse than that.

Geordi entered from the hallway. "Forgive me, Commander, but I'm not sure I should be away from engineering."

"I don't anticipate being on the station very long, Geordi," Riker said as he stepped onto the transporter pad. "And what you see there might be able to help us on the *Enterprise*."

Geordi climbed onto the pad.

Riker glanced over his shoulder. Data was in place. "Energize."

His body dissolved into multicolored light. Then, almost instantly, he was rematerializing on Brundage Station. The air felt hot and sticky.

It smelled of sulfur.

A shiver ran down Riker's spine.

The lights were on, but a thin haze of smoke and mist floated in the air, reminiscent of the smoke in the holodeck nightclubs where Data had once practiced his awful comedy routines.

The anxiety Riker had felt since that morning rose, catching in his throat like a bone. The hair on the back of his neck rose. Yet, except for the smell and the smoke, nothing looked out of place.

He pulled out his phaser. "Data, analyze the air for me. What am I smelling?"

Data sniffed, not even needing his tricorder. "The air has a sulfuric component that is slowly fading. The humidity is at ninety-seven percent, and the temperature is ten degrees above normal. I do not detect any trace of fire. The smoke mixed with the humid mist seems to be from some sort of heat weapon."

Riker nodded. Data's matter-of-fact answer enabled Riker to put some of the anxiety aside. Alongside Riker, Geordi also had his phaser out. He then removed his tricorder. It hummed as it ran through its routine.

"If I didn't know better," Geordi said, "I would think we were in the steam baths of Risa. But I couldn't tell you what's causing the effect. My readings show the environmental controls are working normally."

"Risa smells better than this," Riker said. "Draw your weapon, Data."

"Aye, sir," Data said, his tone puzzled. He obviously saw no threat.

They stepped off the transporter pad as one unit, but moving in three slightly different directions.

"The life-sign readings are coming from that corridor," Geordi said, indicating the door with his phaser. "They're faint."

"Are you getting anything else?" Riker asked as he made his way to the door.

Geordi shook his head.

Data moved quicker than they did. The door opened automatically. Riker stopped, but Data went on as if nothing were wrong. Riker hadn't felt this tentative since he was a cadet at the academy.

He glanced at Geordi, who also hadn't moved. "You feel it too," Riker said softly.

Geordi nodded. "Something terrible happened here. And I don't much like it."

"Over here!" Data said from outside the door.

Riker took a deep breath of the oppressive air, and hurried toward the door. There a young officer—the same officer who had faced the Furies on the transmission—leaned against the wall like a broken toy soldier. His head lolled to the side.

Data was running his tricorder over the boy. "I see no obvious wounds," Data said, "but his life signs are very weak."

Riker knelt beside the boy and saw that his eyes

were open. "Lieutenant," Riker said. "Lieutenant Young?"

"I don't think he can see you," Geordi said. He crouched beside them, observing Young's eyes.

"Is he blind?" Data asked.

Geordi shook his head. "Probably catatonic."

Riker slapped his comm badge. "Riker to *Enterprise.*"

Lieutenant Young jerked away from Riker's voice and covered his head. Only a croaking came from his throat as he tried to scream.

Young's action made Riker shiver.

"Enterprise here. Go ahead, Number One."

"We found Lieutenant Young. He appears to be in shock. I suggest we beam him directly to sickbay."

"Acknowledged, Number One." As Captain Picard's voice faded, multicolored light enveloped Young. Young cringed even more as he disappeared.

"He was not injured," Data said again.

"Yes, he was, Data," Geordi said softly. He stood and went to the computer access panel near the door.

Riker took out his own tricorder, and checked its readings. With Young gone, the three men were alone on the station.

Or so it seemed.

The hair still standing on the back of Riker's neck told him otherwise.

"Geordi, how long will it take you to download the station's records?"

"Only a minute," Geordi said.

"Data, come with me," Riker said. "Let's see what else we can find."

The smoke and the damp, warm mist grew thicker

the deeper they went into the corridor. The carpet was burned in several places as if this part of the station had been on fire.

Writing covered one wall, red writing, as if it had been done in blood.

"Can you read that, Data?" Riker asked.

Data frowned at it. "I believe it is ancient Hebrew. However, it is written in reverse, as if the writer either did not know the proper sequence of letters or—"

"It might have been intentional. What does it say?"

"It is not a message or a warning."

"Then what's its purpose?" Riker asked.

"I believe," Data said, "it is a statement of the powerlessness of Yahweh. It would have horrified the ancient Hebrews. But these words have not been considered blasphemous for at least two, almost three, millennia. I find it curious that they think this will frighten our crew."

"Some ancient imagery terrified some of the old *Enterprise* crew," Riker said. "Kirk theorized these images trigger buried memories—"

"I am familiar with the theory, Commander, although I do not understand why imagery would have an effect and words would not."

"Neither do I," Riker said. The crawly feeling from the back of his neck had worked its way down his spine. He continued down the hall, stepping over the burned patches.

Around a shallow corner was a sight that made him freeze. A red pitchfork-like instrument stood upside down, stuck on a pile of bones. Riker swallowed. "Data?"

Data scanned the bones with his tricorder. "These

bones are real, Commander. They belong to two human males. The red pitchfork has no non-decorative function that I can ascertain."

Riker closed his eyes. He didn't want to think about how these men had died.

"I will run a DNA scan?" Data asked.

Riker nodded. "Be careful. I think we should avoid touching the display. We need to be as careful as we can."

He wiped a hand on his forehead. The corridor had grown hotter and the mist thicker.

He pulled out his own tricorder and scanned, but no life-forms registered. He stepped around the pile of bones and moved on.

Ahead was another corner in the hall. He was almost afraid to move forward, but somehow managed to push himself around the corner—

—and there he stopped, his gaze locked on the eyes of the station's only female crew member.

She was standing in a circle of flame. Her hair had burned away long since, but her flesh was intact—at least the flesh that was visible. The flames rose around her like an inverted waterfall. The glimpses it gave of her face revealed chapped lips, a slightly reddish cast to her skin, and empty eyes.

"Data?" Riker said.

Data stepped past Riker instantly and approached the burning woman. He stopped near her, just outside the ring of flame. "She is dead, Commander, but I do not believe the flames killed her. Like Lieutenant Young, she has no life-threatening injuries."

Riker nodded, his feet rooted to the spot.

Data did not seem to notice his commander's

distress. "The flames seem to be shooting from the floor, but there is no mechanism creating this illusion. I could get closer—"

"No!" Riker said. He cleared his throat, forced the overwhelming anxiety down. "This might be the trap Worf suspected."

"I rather doubt that, sir," Data said. "My study this morning leads me to conclude that this is the eternal hellfire and damnation that Earth's Judeo-Christian ethic speaks of. It would make sense, since this officer was raised within that tradition."

"And she was literally scared to death," Riker said. He tapped his comm badge. The sooner they left this place, the happier he would be. "Are you finished, Geordi?"

"Almost," Geordi said. "I'll have everything in a moment."

"Excellent." Riker whirled and moved back down the corridor, heading toward Geordi's position as quickly as he could.

"Commander—" Data said, hurrying to catch up. "Commander, we have yet to explore the entire station."

"I don't think we should stay here any longer, Data," Riker said. He wasn't sure he could stay here much longer.

"But, sir, our duty—"

"Are there other life signs?"

"No, sir."

"Then I don't think it's our duty to go any farther into this station. Captain Picard made it clear that we would get the information and then leave."

"Aye, sir. I had thought that—"

"Save it, Mr. Data," Riker said, more harshly than he intended. He passed the bones and didn't look at them. His instincts had been right; this was a hall of death. And the Furies were cunning. They knew that by creating a mystery around the deaths, they would engage the imagination.

His nerves were frayed by the time he reached Geordi. Before Geordi could say anything, Riker hit his comm badge. "Three to beam up."

And as the beam took them, he didn't feel relief. He felt as if he had gazed into the Pit, and saw a small corner of the future.

His future.

Chapter Six

THE SHIPS HADN'T MOVED. But they knew the *Enterprise* was at Brundage Station.

They had to.

The Furies were not insanely violent. Kirk had recorded that. History proved that. He had talked to them, reasoned with them.

Unless they had changed over the decades.

Picard felt as if he were being set up.

But that was his mission. His was the first ship on site. He glanced at Ensign Eckley at the helm this shift. She was a good pilot. Not the best, but one of the best. Good enough to allow his other crew members to fill different roles.

Deanna had left the bridge. Worf glowered at the screen from his position at the security console. Picard was pacing.

He couldn't seem to stop pacing.

Each second the away team had been on Brundage Station had been an eternity. Even now, for Riker to return to the bridge and report seemed as if it were taking forever.

Finally the turbolift opened and Riker strode onto the bridge. His face was white and sweat streaks marred his skin. Not the streaks from healthy exercise that Picard had seen earlier. No. This had been caused by something else entirely. And his passage left a faint odor behind it. Something familiar and yet odd.

Sulfur?

Sulfur.

And the creature who had spoken to Lieutenant Young had looked like a medieval devil.

So that was what the Furies were about this time. Devils and hell. Picard's European past. He was prepared. He would be able to handle that.

Geordi La Forge had already returned to engineering. Data followed Riker off the turbolift. Data's uniform had dark smudges on it, as if he had rubbed against soot.

The mission clearly had not gone as planned. Something about Riker's behavior warned Picard that this discussion should not be held before an audience.

"In my ready room," Picard said. He crossed the bridge and entered his room. Riker followed, eyes averted. Data slipped in just as the door closed.

Picard crossed behind his desk. "What so disturbed you, Will?"

Riker brought his head up, startled at the question. He glanced at Data, who was regarding him as if

Riker were an unfamiliar life-form. "I—ah—those deaths were gruesome, sir."

"Tell me about them," Picard said.

Riker opened his mouth, closed it, and then turned away. Data tilted his head. His gaze met Picard's.

"Mr. Data?"

"As you suspected, sir, the Furies are using ancient religions and mythologies to base a psychological attack. In this case they mixed medieval Earth ideas of hell with even older damnation imagery. Liberal use of fire, smells, and—"

"She was burned alive, sir," Riker said, his voice unsteady. "Only her flesh hadn't charred. I think she died of fright. The others were bones. Just bones."

"And the survivor?"

"Didn't have a mark on him, sir. We sent him to sickbay."

"Geordi has the logs in engineering. Someone might want to view them." Riker's voice broke slightly. "But I won't."

"No need for you to, Number One." Picard tented his fingers on his desk and leaned forward. "But we only have a moment and I need you tell me what unnerved you so badly."

Riker shook his head. "I don't know, sir." Picard recognized the underlying anxiety in Riker's tone. No officer liked losing control, even a small portion of control, and losing that control for no reason at all was even worse. "The station just felt bad, as if it were an evil place."

He shook his head and wiped a hand through his dark hair. "I've been trying to figure it out since I've returned. I've seen worse, Captain. Much worse. But nothing has ever *felt* like this before. It was as if, just by breathing the air, I was taking evil inside me."

"Mr. Data?" Picard needed a clear perspective.

"Commander Riker is correct, sir. We have seen much worse. The loss of life, tragic though it was, seemed stylized and deliberate rather than calculated to horrify and disgust. Yet from the moment we materialized, both the commander and Geordi appeared to be on edge. I am at a loss for an explanation."

Riker squared his shoulders at that description and clasped his hands behind his back. Data's analysis of the station seemed to calm Riker. "My best guess, sir," Riker said, "is that Geordi and I were both raised in the culture that produced those images of hell. I think humans like us were the intended targets, and I think we felt that as an underlying unease."

"What do you think, Mr. Data?"

"It would fit with what I observed, sir. I must note that both the commander and Geordi were able to perform their duties despite their"—Data glanced at Riker as he chose the next word—"their, ah, discomfort."

"Thank you," Picard said. "Data, return to the bridge. I want you to scan the records that Mr. La Forge brought back from Brundage Station. See how the Furies accomplished their attack, and also keep an eye open for anything that we can use."

"Aye, sir," Data said. He started toward the door. Riker followed.

"Number One, stay for a moment."

Riker paused, his eyes down. Picard had never seen his first officer so off-balance before. He needed Riker.

Riker had to be on his feet and thinking clearly before they faced the Furies.

"Will," Picard said softly. "You performed your duties."

"But that fear—it shouldn't have happened at all, Captain," Riker said. "I was prepared. I shouldn't have felt anything."

Picard smiled. "If only it were that easy, Will. You cannot stop the feelings. You must keep them from overwhelming you. The information that you gave me is critical, and your emotional reaction even more so. The Furies may use many tools against us, from appearance to smell. I would have been uncomfortable there. The fact that you completed your mission despite your feelings gives me hope for all of us."

He rounded the desk and clasped Riker on the shoulder. Riker started, then gave Picard a shocked look.

"Good work, Number One. Return to the bridge. I'll join you momentarily."

Riker nodded, then left.

Picard took a deep breath. The descriptions of the station were horrible, but not terrifying. He had seen worse—suffered worse—himself. Yet he could not discount his first officer's reaction. Riker had also gone through a lot in his tenure at Starfleet. Smells, and death, should not have unnerved him this badly. They never had in the past.

Kirk's description of the Furies was right.

But Kirk had kept his emotions in check, and so would Picard.

Admiral Kirschbaum had told him to negotiate.

Kirk's records placed the Furies as a threat even though he had negotiated and even considered the captain of the Fury ship a friend. But this time the Furies had come through the wormhole with five ships. More than one, but clearly not an entire fleet. They still wanted conquest. The attack on the station was only a reminder of what they could do. A warning.

A calling card.

Picard hoped beyond hope that was the way it was, but his heart told him he was wrong.

He strode back onto the bridge.

Data had returned to his post at the science station. Material was flowing rapidly across the screen before him. Commander Riker had taken his seat near the captain's chair. He looked calmer.

"Ensign Eckley," Picard said to the helmsman as he made his way to his command post. "Take us within communications range of those ships."

"Aye, sir," Eckley said.

Picard noticed Riker's fist tighten. The tension on the bridge grew. Picard sat and leaned back in his seat, not allowing himself to move with the mood shift.

Perhaps all the study of the Furies at the Academy had been wrong. Perhaps Starfleet crew members would approach the attack with a more open mind if they hadn't been told that the Furies were so powerful. Despite generations of study, no one completely understood the human mind. Perhaps the warnings had intensified the feelings of danger instead of alleviating them.

"We're within range, sir."

"All stop." Picard stood and tugged on his shirt front. "Hail them."

He had seen the images from Brundage Station. He had seen his own trusted first officer's reaction to the mess the Furies left behind them. He knew what he was in for.

"Sir," Worf said, his deep voice booming across the bridge. "We have a response to our hail."

"On screen."

The bridge seemed abnormally silent, as if the bridge crew were holding their breath. Picard felt as if he had contained his emotions in a small bottle buried deep within his stomach.

He was as ready as he could ever be.

The screen flickered to life. Picard had to fight an involuntary urge to step backward. The creature facing him was both familiar and unfamiliar. It had ram's horns and a long snout. Its scarlet skin and piggy eyes matched portraits of the devil made on Earth, matching illuminated manuscript drawings he had seen as a boy in Paris museums. If he had time to lay a wager, he would bet that the creature before him had the body of a goat yet stood on its hind legs, had cloven hooves instead of feet, and had no tail at all.

His stomach felt as if it were about to burst.

"I am Captain Jean-Luc Picard of the *Starship Enterprise*."

The creature laughed. Maggots swarmed out of its open mouth. Its teeth were long and sharp. Saliva dripped from them. "Captain," it said, its voice a warm caress that was somehow more hideous than the voice he had expected. "I know who you are. I

54

even know of your Federation of Planets. But you do not know who I am. You have faced my people, but not my kind."

Picard took a deep breath. He would not play this guessing game, but suddenly he couldn't think of any other response. Everything he had planned to say had fled from his mind. The emotions he had bottled away were straining at their prison.

"I," the creature said, its bass tones reverberating all the way down to Picard's toes, "am fear."

Its words echoed in the silent bridge as the screen went dark.

Already they were seeping through: images of himself . . .

. . . locked alone in a room near the vineyard, the smell of fresh grapes and sunshine taunting him . . .

. . . alone on Casius II, his shuttlecraft in pieces around him, night with its poisonous chill approaching; and naked in the Borg hive, imprisoned in one of their devices, a needle longer than his finger heading straight for his temple . . .

He wrenched himself out of the memory.

He was here.

On the *Enterprise.*

Safe.

The seeping fear was still there, but slowly, as if a spider had dropped a web over his emotions, his control returned. He knew the control was as flimsy as a spider's web and would break just as easily. But it gave him something else to work with.

He blinked, turned, and finally saw the bridge before him.

The sight shocked him.

Riker sat in his chair, his elbows braced on his knees, his head buried in his hands. He was shivering.

Ensign Eckley had her arms wrapped around her head. She had fallen to the floor and she appeared to have passed out.

Ensign Wilcox was sobbing, the harsh guttural sobs of a man who had never cried before.

Ensign Ikel was pounding on the turbolift door as if he were trying to escape the room.

The big surprise, though, was Lieutenant Worf. The devil had no place in his tradition, yet he stared at the empty screen, his dark, foreboding features the color of Ferengi grub worms. He seemed frozen in place.

"Captain, I have finished the analysis. . . ." Data swiveled his chair, and stopped speaking as he saw the condition of the bridge crew. A tiny frown furrowed his normally wrinkleless face.

"It seems," he said, his gaze meeting Picard's, "that I have missed something."

Picard took another deep breath and let the fine web of his self-control strengthen just a little bit more. "I think we may be lucky that you did," he said.

Data frowned, and for some reason Picard found that very reassuring.

Deanna Troi sat on the bed in her quarters, her door locked. Her comm badge rested on the table in the main room. She could hear it, but had chosen not to respond. Already she had gotten calls from fifteen crew members, no doubt wanting to discuss the anxiety they had been feeling since the *Enterprise* had come to this area near the Brundage Station.

The anxiety she was feeling was threatening to overwhelm her.

A Betazoid, her mind said with the voice of her mother, *knows how to control the impact of the emotions of others.*

"I know, Mother," Deanna said. She gripped her knees and went through a calming ritual that had helped her in times past. Usually she handled these overwhelming crew emotions better than she was now. She suspected her reaction was due to the strength of the emotions.

And they would only get stronger, magnified within her own self.

Unless you get control, Deanna. I don't recognize this lack of control anywhere in my family. It must come from your father.

Deanna never heard the voice of her mother in her own head. Unless, of course, her mother was nearby.

"Computer, is my mother on board the *Enterprise?*"

"Lwaxana Troi is not aboard this ship."

"Computer please check again."

"Lwaxana Troi is not aboard this ship."

Deanna nodded. Her anxiety level was high. She hadn't made up her mother's voice since she was a very young girl. Then that had been normal. A child always heard voices where there were none. It was the task of the Betazoid to learn the difference between a projected voice and an imagined one.

Deanna stood, her skirts falling about her legs. Her mother's voice—real or imagined—was right. Deanna needed control.

She left the bedroom, grabbed her comm badge, and put it on. Her research with Data showed that the Furies had not encountered Betazoids. The Furies would have no knowledge of Betazed mythology. Only her human side would be affected, and she could control that much.

The problem she would have in any encounter with the Furies would be the shipboard reaction. But she suspected, and Data hypothesized, that the Furies had come through this sector long before the original *Enterprise* encountered them.

Her mother's planet had no history of them.

None.

That would give her strength.

If you can keep everyone else out of your mind, her mother's voice said.

"You leave first, Mother," Deanna snapped. She didn't need this distraction. Her mother always made her nervous. . . .

She paused. *Her mother made her nervous.* Deanna sighed. So even when she was trying to block the low-level anxiety from the ship, it appeared in the form of her mother.

Deanna would go to her counseling offices. She had practiced control there more than she had in her own rooms. She was amazed she hadn't thought of that immediately.

"Computer," she said, "please block all non-emergency calls. I will set appointments after this crisis has ended."

"Affirmative," the computer said.

There. That part at least was settled. No one on the

ship had the luxury to discuss their emotional difficulties. They simply had to live through them.

Just as she would.

She felt better now. The control she had been seeking had returned. She started for the door.

And fell forward as a wave of cold hit her as hard as a physical blow. The cold was full of voices—screaming, shouting, babbling—and imagery:

A woman whose head was covered with snakes.

A creature with maggots for eyes.

A giant Klingon, his teeth covered with blood.

Mixed in with those were a hundred others, less prominent, but as forceful.

And behind it all, her mother's voice.

Deanna, you need control. Deanna—

But she had no control. Her mother would have had no control. There was too much. Too much for anyone to handle all at once.

Deanna fought the cold back, the voices back, but the images kept coming—   A great dragon, spitting fire.

A Romulan, poised over her with a disruptor.

A Craxithesus, screaming its blood cry.

More and more and more.

—She couldn't stop them, and as she fought, she grew weaker, and weaker.

The images crowded in on her until her senses overloaded.

She could fight no more.

Chapter Seven

LIEUTENANT SAM REDBAY straddled a chair in engineering. He held a laser under his arm as he pulled apart the panel before him. Just his luck to be in engineering instead of on the bridge during what promised to be the biggest event of his career. But he had told personnel that if they assigned him to a starship he would work in any department at any time, and he had always had an aptitude for engineering.

And, to be fair, he liked the work. Although he liked working the helm better.

But Lieutenant Tam was down with the Xotic flu, a deadly (and fortunately not very communicable) virus that damaged the internal organs if not monitored properly. And Dr. Crusher had ordered complete bed rest.

Tam had contacted La Forge when the crisis started, and he gave her some sort of mental puzzle to work on from her sickbed. If it had been Redbay, he would have crawled to his battle station, virus be damned.

Still, if he had to be somewhere outside of the action, he would rather be in engineering than anywhere else. Geordi La Forge ran a tight section. The equipment was always in top condition. The *Enterprise* functioned at maximum capacity, and everything the crew did only made it better.

Like the work Redbay was doing now. La Forge believed, based on the things he had read and some things he had noticed in his trip to Brundage Station, that some of the Furies' powers over human fears might be artificial and therefore could be effectively blocked. Redbay had already worked on a shield oscillator so that unusual frequencies would be scrambled. Now he was modifying the viewscreens to minimize intentional distortions.

The job should theoretically take two people eight hours.

He had an hour to finish it.

Alone.

The rest of the engineering staff were working on similar tasks. A few were modifying the warp engines—for what he did not know—and La Forge himself was in a Jeffries tube, adjusting the internal sensors.

They would be ready when the Furies struck.

If they struck.

Redbay had his doubts about that. His own personal opinion, based on some historical study, was that

Captain James T. Kirk was a bit of an exaggerator. No one, no matter what his position and no matter what the tenor of his times, could have been involved in so many important events in the history of the sector.

Redbay's history professor at the Academy had ridiculed that conclusion, pointing out that the history records clearly showed Kirk's involvement.

This, of course, would be the test. Kirk and his crew were the only ones who left a record of the Furies' visit. The Klingons had been suspiciously silent about the entire encounter. And from the punishment they took, Redbay could understand why.

His hand was getting tired from holding the laser in place. He still had some tweaking to do. With luck, he would be able to get the task done in the time allotted. If it hadn't been for the prime condition of the *Enterprise*'s systems, the job really would have taken him the full eight hours.

Then, suddenly, his heart rate increased, his hands started shaking, and his fingers lost their grip on the laser. It slipped from his mouth and clattered on the console, denting the surface.

He dropped his tools and grabbed for the laser, knowing that the monsters under his bed were going to get him, they were going to kill him, like they had killed his father and his mother and the entire colony.

He had to hide now.

Now!

Hide! Right now!

He slid under the console and drew his knees up to his chest, but that didn't drive the feeling away. The monsters were made of light, multicolored light, and they burned everything they touched. He had seen his father die that way, and his mother had made him run—

A man was on his back, phaser clutched in both hands, pushing, pushing, pushing his way toward Redbay using his heels as propulsion, eyes focused on a point near the ceiling. The man was wearing a Starfleet uniform (Starfleet? how did they get here?), and he was moaning as he moved.

A long drawn-out scream echoed from a Jeffries tube (a what?), and two ensigns were lying on the floor, each a shivering mass of flesh.

They had to hide. Didn't they know they had to hide? If they were in the open, the light would get them and—

and—

Starfleet didn't belong on Nyo Colony. The colony had broken with the Federation. That's why so many people died. Because they had no one to turn to for help. That's why Redbay joined Starfleet, so that he could help people who needed it.

Redbay joined.

He was in Starfleet.

His parents had died a long, long time ago.

He peered out from under the console. The man in the Starfleet uniform (Transporter Chief Anderson) was still pushing himself with his legs, moving on his back, aiming his phaser at shadows.

Redbay was in engineering on the *Starship Enterprise*. Getting ready to face the Furies.

Who terrified their opponents by manipulating their emotions.

Terror.

He had only felt this kind of terror once in his life. The day his parents died.

Only once.

His parents had died thirty years ago.

Thirty.

Years.

Thirty.

He kept repeating that inside his head, over and over.

He had been modulating the ship's screens. He had no reason to be so frightened.

None.

But his limbs were shaking.

He eased out from under the console, the terror still a part of him, but slowly coming under control. If he kept his mind focused the terror would always be under control

He had learned that at age six, living alone for a month on Nyo before a passing freighter had picked up the automated distress signal.

Redbay kept his gaze on Chief Anderson—no sense in startling a panicked man—and slowly stood, his legs trembling.

The surface of the console was dented where the laser initially hit, but *again,* none of the important sensors were damaged.

The damage all seemed to be internal—within the engineering staff.

Then La Forge rolled out of the Jeffries tube, slapping himself as though he were on fire. He landed on his back, and gasped as the air left his lungs. His hands slapped their way up to his face. When they reached his VISOR, he stopped.

Anderson hit his head against the console, yelped, and aimed his phaser at the wall.

Redbay didn't move. He wasn't going to move until Anderson put the phaser down.

La Forge removed the VISOR and sat up, leaning against the opening of the tube. He was breathing hard, but he seemed to be calmer.

Anderson put his phaser away.

Redbay let out breath he hadn't even realized he was holding. Slowly he made his way to La Forge. La Forge's face looked odd without the VISOR. Redbay had never seen his eyes before, didn't realize that they were a milky white. The eyes didn't focus on him.

"M-Mr. La Forge?" Redbay's voice sounded strangled. He cleared his throat. "Sir?"

With a hand not yet completely steady, La Forge put his VISOR back on. "Lieutenant."

He sounded calm. If Redbay hadn't seen him fall out of the Jeffries tube in a panic, he would have thought that La Forge had felt nothing.

"I can see two crew members who still haven't controlled themselves," Redbay said, letting La Forge know that his panic was not unique. "Anderson seems to be coming out of it. I haven't been able to get to the warp drive to see what's happening there."

"Great," La Forge said, and he didn't have to explain what he meant by that. If La Forge had panicked and fallen out of a Jeffries tube, and Redbay had panicked and allowed a laser to damage a console, then what kind of damage happened to the warp core?

La Forge pulled himself to his feet. "Engineering to bridge," he said as he stood.

"Go ahead, Mr. La Forge."

Redbay found the captain's normal response unusually reassuring. But La Forge frowned. He had worked with Picard a long time. He might have heard something in the captain's voice that Redbay hadn't.

"Captain." La Forge paused and glanced around, then took a deep breath and continued. "Something pretty strange just happened down here. I don't know how to describe it. We all seemed to panic for no reason at all. Two of my ensigns are still huddled in terror on the floor, and I don't know what's going on near the warp core. There might be some systems damage. I'll need help from the bridge in running a systems check."

"That isn't possible at the moment, Mr. La Forge."

Now Redbay heard it too. There seemed to be an abnormal amount of caution in the captain's tone, as if he were choosing his words too carefully.

"Then, sir, give us five minutes before attempting to use any major system. I need to check—"

"Mr. La Forge," the captain interrupted as if he hadn't heard La Forge at all. "Did you have the screens on during the last transmission?"

La Forge glanced at Redbay. Redbay shook his head. He had been working on the screens, not watching them.

"No, sir," La Forge said.

"Fascinating." The captain's comment was soft, as if he were mulling that piece of information.

The silence seem to stretch too long. Finally La Forge said, "Captain?"

"Mr. La Forge." Picard's voice seemed somewhat stronger. "We have a problem that extends beyond engineering and the bridge. We must assume that the entire ship has felt this wave of terror. Repair what you can, Mr. La Forge, but remain at your posts."

"Yes, sir," La Forge said.

"Geordi," Picard said, his voice lower, almost as if he were asking a favor. "Get your crew on their feet again, if you can. We need to discover where this feeling is coming from, as quickly as possible."

"Lieutenant Redbay and I are already on our feet," La Forge said, "and Anderson seems to have regained control as well. Between the three of us, we should be able to get the rest of engineering in order."

"Good," Picard said. "I need a report as soon as you can get it to me."

"Aye, sir," La Forge said.

Redbay swallowed convulsively. It was taking most of his strength to stand beside La Forge and look calm.

La Forge's hand went to his VISOR again, then dropped to his side. "I suspect we don't have much time."

"I suspect you're right," Redbay said. "I think those of us who can work should. If we find a way to block whatever is causing this, the others will come around immediately."

La Forge glanced at his crew members. One ensign was still huddled in a fetal position, but the other one was sitting up, his skin green, his eyes glazed. He was tracking, though. Redbay suspected he had looked like that only moments before.

"I'll scan," La Forge said. "You run diagnostics. Let's see how fast we can find the source of this."

Redbay nodded. He liked being busy. Being busy

kept his mind off that feeling of terror gnawing at the lining of his stomach. He went back to the console and picked up his tools. Beneath the control, beyond the terror, he had the awful feeling that something was missing.

Something that should have guided them all.

He bent over another console and started the diagnostics.

Then he realized what was wrong.

No one had ordered a red alert.

If Picard was right, then the entire crew had been hit with a bolt of fear, a literal assault on the senses.

A clear attack and Picard had not called a red alert.

He had probably been too shaken to think of it.

And that worried Redbay even more.

Chapter Eight

SICKBAY GLEAMED.

The extra beds were lined against the wall, the emergency equipment was out on tables, and extra medical tricorders hung from pegs near the door. Beverly Crusher had even ordered her assistants to place the research tubes into medical storage so that they could use the experiment area during any emergency that might arise. The handful of patients, three sick with the Xotic flu, were in the farthest wing of sickbay, tended by one nurse who was instructed to watch the monitors for any fluctuations.

Beverly tucked a strand of red hair behind her ear and looked at the readings on the diagnostic bed one more time. She had prepared her trauma team, not her research team. After working on Lieutenant

Young, however, she wondered if she had made the right decision.

Lieutenant Young was still wrapped in the diagnostic bed, only his head and feet visible above the equipment. Aside from an odd series of bruises across his chest, arms, and ankles, he had suffered no obvious physical wounds. Yet he was nearly comatose.

She had thought, when he first beamed up, that he had had serious internal injuries, or some type of head wound. But as she examined him, then stabilized him, she discovered his lack of physical injury.

Obvious physical injury. She had to keep reminding herself that the key word here was "obvious." Lieutenant Young—who looked, in some ways, younger than her son Wesley—was dying.

And she could do nothing about it until she determined the cause.

Two of her assistants were running double-check scans on his blood and urine. She was also having them run DNA tests and tests for obscure viral infections: for anything that would cause Young's abnormally high blood pressure, his increased adrenaline and endorphin readings, and his extra white-blood-cell count.

The thing she didn't tell her assistants was that she was afraid she knew the cause.

One of her hobbies was the history of medicine throughout the known worlds. It fascinated her that Vulcan developed the art of acupuncture during roughly the same developmental period Earth did—even though the planets were not in communication at that time and the cultures were in different states of growth.

Terminology also interested her: the phrase "in good humor" once meant "in good health" because Terrans once believed that the body was filled with "humors" and that if those humors were in balance, then a person was healthy. She didn't believe in humors any more than she believed in using leeches to bleed a cancer patient, but she did know that some ancient diagnoses held a basis in fact.

She ran a cool hand over Young's forehead. No fever, yet his skin was damp and clammy to the touch. His eyes were open, but they didn't see her. Instead they focused on the ceiling. Occasionally he would moan and cringe. And when he did, his heart rate increased, his breath stopped in his throat, and his blood pressure rose.

She could bring the levels down, but she couldn't predict when the situation would repeat.

And she knew, as clearly as she knew her own name, that Lieutenant Young's ill health was being caused by something within his own mind.

In the terms of the medieval physicians of Earth, Lieutenant Robert Young was being frightened to death.

Literally.

And search as she might for a physical cause—an implanted chip, a stimulant in the brain stem, a chemical trigger in his bloodstream—she could find nothing.

She suspected that he had seen something he could not live with, and his conscious mind, overloaded, was trying to cope in the only way it could. It was overloading his body, trying to force it to shut down.

And it was up to her to stop that.

She dabbed sweat off Young's forehead. Sometimes she felt no better than those medieval physicians who believed that humors governed the body. There were parts of the body—human, Vulcan, Klingon, it didn't matter—that no one understood.

This was one of them.

She needed Deanna. If anyone could help this boy, Deanna could.

Beverly reached for her comm badge when suddenly a wave of terror filled her. The feeling was so intense that it knocked her to her knees. She banged her head on the diagnostic table as she fell.

The boy was going to die.

They all were going to die.

And she could do nothing. She was perfectly helpless. As helpless as she had been the day Jean-Luc arrived with the news that her husband was dead.

That she would raise Wesley alone.

The ship would be filled with a mental plague, causing everyone to die of fright, and she, a trained physician, would have to stand by.

Helplessly.

Her head hurt.

The beginning of the plague.

She knew it.

Bobby Young was only the beginning, and now it had passed to her. Soon she would lie on a diagnostic table while her assistants fluttered over her. Then they would fall, one by one, victim to this unnamed terror—

Someone behind her screamed.

The plague was spreading.

She put a hand to her head, near the source of the pain, and felt—

A lump.

It hurt to the touch, hurt even worse when she pressed on it, making the headache increase.

Something crashed behind her.

She whirled.

One of her assistants—she couldn't see who—had made a white flag out of God knows what, and was waving it from below one of the examining tables.

A white flag.

She frowned. Then giggled, despite her terror. A white flag. No one recognized a white flag anymore. It once meant surrender. Save the bearer from harm.

Save the bearer from harm.

Cautiously, she peered above the diagnostic table. Young was writhing within his confines, his eyes rolling in his head.

Young.

Save the bearer from harm.

She glanced around the room.

Except for her assistants, she was alone.

The flag waved, slowly, like a metronome.

Tick.

Save the

Tick.

bearer from

Tick.

harm.

Her throat was dry. She had never felt such terror in her life. Something was wrong. Something was—

Lieutenant Young choked.

She rose by instinct, opened his mouth, and cleared

the passageway. Her fingers were shaking. She couldn't concentrate. She forgot what she was trying to do.

Save the bearer from harm.

That was her duty. Her oath.

I swear by Apollo the physician, by Aesculapius, Hygeia, and Panacea

His throat was clear.

and I take to witness all the gods, all the goddesses, to keep according to my ability and my judgment the following Oath:

But his tongue was bleeding.

I will prescribe regimen for the good of my patients

She cleansed his tongue, moved it aside, and propped up his head.

according to my ability and my judgment and never do harm to anyone.

He was breathing regularly again.

His eyelashes were fluttering.

And her terror was subsiding. Or more accurately, she had it under control.

Never do harm to anyone.

And it was the oath, the Hippocratic oath, that had saved her. Hippocrates, Father of Medicine, a Greek physician who came from a famous family of priest physicians, and who wrote more than seventy treatises on medicine . . .

Knowledge.

It was knowledge that was keeping her calm. Her mind could overcome anything. Hadn't Dr. Quince told her that during her internship on Delos IV? Her mind was more powerful than any drug. More powerful than anything.

Even fear.

She was standing without assistance. Even in the middle of that terror, she had managed to help Lieutenant Young.

Now she had to help her assistants because she needed them.

She peered over the examining table. Ensign Cassidy was sitting below, both hands clutching the white flag, which was still waving back and forth.

Beverly swallowed. "Etta," she said. "Etta, it's Beverly. You're in sickbay. Put down the flag. You're safe."

Ensign Cassidy looked up, her round face pale with fear. "Don't let them get me, Doctor," she whispered.

"They won't, Ensign. No one is here. Captain Picard warned us this would happen. There are Furies outside. Remember the Furies?"

Ensign Cassidy nodded.

"Use your mind, Ensign. Overcome the fear. Put it aside. Remember your medical training. Your fears don't matter. Your actions do."

In every house where I come I will enter only for the good of my patients. Beverly shivered. The fear was there, below the surface. But she could control it.

Ensign Cassidy lowered the flag. "What's causing this?" she whispered.

"Something from outside us." Beverly took a deep breath. "I need you to focus the others. Remind them of their tasks as medical personnel. Even Lieutenant Young can feel this, and he doesn't seem to feel anything else."

She stopped, the fear caught in her throat. A real fear this time.

Deanna!

"Computer," she said, not caring that the fear filled her voice. "Locate Counselor Troi."

"She is in her quarters."

Deanna. Who was sensitive to everyone's mood. Who could feel what the entire ship was feeling.

Terror like this overloaded a human. Lieutenant Bobby Young was dying from it. Imagine what it would do to Deanna.

Beverly turned to Cassidy. "Keep an eye on our patient. Contact me if there's any problem."

Ensign Cassidy blinked. Her expression was clearer. "I'll be all right," she said.

"Good," Beverly said. That made it easier for her to leave.

And she had to. She had to get to Deanna.

Beverly headed out the door at a run, spurred on by fear. But not the fear sent by the Furies. This fear was for her friend's life.

Chapter Nine

"I SIMPLY DO NOT understand, sir," Data said. "Did I miss some subtle message in your contact with the Furies?"

His head jerked as it turned, looking at the bridge crew. Lieutenant Worf still stared at the screen. Riker brought his head up, an expression of grim determination on his face. Ensign Iket had stopped pounding on the turbolift door and was holding one hand as if it hurt.

Picard nodded. His fear was still there, but the control he had placed over it grew with each passing moment. "Perhaps, Data, but what you missed was not subtle. It affected the crew's emotions deeply."

"What was it, sir?"

"If we knew that, Mr. Data, we would be able to fight it."

"But you seem unaffected, sir."

Picard smiled. Sometimes Data's innocence on matters emotional was just what Picard needed. Still, he could feel the fear trapped within him, under his control, but only barely. "It affected me, Mr. Data, and I fear—" He paused on the word, checked it, and made sure it was accurate. It was. "I fear that this first attack might be a mild one. For a moment, I felt like Ensign Eckley; and in that extreme terror, no human can think clearly."

Picard looked at Data.

Data was watching him carefully, ignoring the emotional chaos around them.

Picard went on. "There may come a time in our dealings with the Furies when you and you alone will be able to think rationally. I will be counting on you to make the correct decisions. Am I making myself clear, Mr. Data?"

"Yes, sir," Data said in his most solemn voice.

Picard nodded. Having Data aboard—and unaffected by this inexplicable fear—took some of the tension out of Picard's back. Data was a good officer. If the survival of the *Enterprise* and her crew landed on his shoulders, he would make the right choice.

Data's presence, and the guarantee of levelheadedness, also made the next few decisions easier.

"Open a shipwide channel, Mr. Worf."

Worf did not break his gaze from the screen. Data watched him, head tilting in puzzlement.

"Mr. Worf," Picard said in his most commanding voice.

Worf snapped to attention. His gaze, when he

turned it on Picard, was fierce. But Picard knew that fierceness was a Klingon cover for embarrassment.

"Sir?"

"Open a shipwide channel."

"Yes, sir," Worf said.

Picard glanced at the bridge. Riker was watching him now, and several other members of the bridge crew were taking deep breaths. Ensign Eckley was unconscious, though, and Ensign Iket had sunken to the floor, hand swelling to twice its normal size.

"Channel open, sir."

Picard nodded. He cleared his mind, pushed the fear even farther down, and met Data's gaze. It was essential that Picard sound calm and collected for this announcement. Since Data was the only calm member of the bridge crew, Picard would use him as an anchor.

"To the crew of the *Enterprise,* this is Captain Jean-Luc Picard. We have made contact with the Furies, and in that contact, they have somehow tapped emotions buried deep within us. As we suspected, they hope to prey upon our fears."

He took a deep breath, keeping his gaze on Data's calm face, and went on. "Many of you are in the grip of that fear now. You must master it—and you can master it. Remember that what you are feeling is not coming from within you, but from without. Your fear is artificial. Use that knowledge to subdue the terrors."

Data nodded, understanding what Picard was saying. That calmed Picard even more as he went on. "Return to your stations. I shall be contacting the

Furies again, and this time, they shall see that we are made of much sterner stuff."

Picard signed off. Riker was staring at him. Data stood, and opened his mouth as if to speak. But Worf spoke first.

"With all due respect, sir, it was your contact with the Furies that precipitated the attack. Do you believe that another contact is wise considering we do not even know the nature or the power of their weapon?"

"It is the Klingon way to face one's fear, is it not, Mr. Worf?"

"Klingons believe, sir, that one must respect one's fears. Occasionally a fear is justified."

"I agree. Fear is the most protective of all of our emotions. But it cannot govern our lives or our deeds. It is the strongest Klingons, those who can go beyond their fears, who become great leaders."

Picard had to choose his words carefully here, given the Klingon history with the Furies. Worf probably hadn't yet realized that he was in danger of repeating it.

"It is my belief, Mr. Worf," Picard continued, "that you are one of your people's great leaders. I have seen you face events that would have destroyed lesser Klingons."

Worf's lips thinned. He clearly understood Picard's implications. "Thank you, sir."

Picard nodded. He turned away from Worf, hoping that his own strength would hold for this next, most crucial action. "Hail the Furies' ship, Mr. Worf."

"Aye, sir."

Riker had stood too. He stayed just out of range of the viewscreen, but he appeared stronger. Perhaps

Picard's conversation with Worf had helped Riker as well.

"They have acknowledged our hail, sir," Worf said.

Picard straightened his shoulders. He had survived torture by the Cardassians. He could survive anything.

"On screen," Picard said.

The devil—the Fury captain—appeared on the screen again.

Picard shuddered, but he kept himself steady. He had to concentrate for the good of the ship. "When we spoke earlier, you said you were familiar with our Federation. That means you know our mission is a peaceful one. We do not believe in war."

"Our records show that you fight it well enough." The creature's voice swept through Picard.

"Of course we do," Picard said. He held himself rigidly, not wanting any sign of fear to show. "We must defend ourselves. But we believe war is a failure of communication."

"War is more than that," the creature said. "War is glory. It is the only way to achieve heaven."

"Heaven" was the term the first Fury's captain had used for this area of space when he spoke to Kirk.

Tiny shivers were running up and down Picard's back. He forced himself to ignore them. "I was sent to negotiate with you. If you want to settle in this area, we will help you."

The creature tilted its head. Its eyes changed color as it moved, and a bit of smoke or mist curled around its horns. "Negotiate? You believe you can negotiate with us?"

The question was a stall. Even through his fear, Picard could sense that. Kirk had tried to negotiate with them. And he had failed in the end.

"Negotiate," Picard repeated. "Our diplomats will meet with yours, we will establish a truce, and then we will see if we can work out some sort of amenable coexistence."

The creature threw its head back and laughed. Maggots flew from its mouth, and fell against its chin, held there by thin strands of green saliva. "Diplomats? We have no diplomats, Picard. We do not believe in them."

The shivers were growing stronger. Picard swallowed them back. He made himself stare at the screen, even though the maggots disgusted him almost as much as the creature terrified him. "Our leaders will speak with yours. If you tell us your purpose in coming to this sector, we will see what we can do to help—"

"You, the Unclean, offering to help us?" The creature's laughter died, and Picard took an involuntary step backward as the Fury captain's eyes seemed to glow red. "Just as you helped our last ship that arrived here? We ruled heaven once and we are returning to rule it again. Then you will do as we want. No negotiating. No diplomats. It is easier our way."

Picard didn't let his mind dwell on what the creature had said. He didn't dare. "In this quadrant," Picard said, "we work together. We are willing to work with you if you let us."

"Be assured you will work with us." The creature raised its hand, revealing long curling fingernails with razor-sharp tips. "Like little puppets on a string. We shall control your every movement. Your every feeling."

The fear increased so that Picard had to grit his teeth to prevent them from chattering.

The creature leaned forward, as if they were the only two beings in the universe. Its red eyes seemed to glow across the distance, cutting at Picard's insides. "And Picard, we will enjoy your every scream."

The screen went dark. Picard staggered backward, stopping just before he reached his chair. He felt as if someone had taken his insides, squeezed them, and then stretched them. His muscles ached, and he longed to close his eyes and never open them again.

Instead, he slumped into his chair. Sweat soaked the back of his shirt. The bridge crew had not dissolved into anxiety. They still controlled themselves. He wondered if that last blast of terror had been directed at him alone.

"Sir?" Riker said, concern evident in his voice.

Picard took a few measured, deep breaths. "Number One, they know how to tap our deepest fears."

"I know, sir," Riker said.

"But it is artificial." Picard was speaking as much for himself as for his first officer, fighting to wrap that band of control around his thoughts again.

He took a deep, measured breath and let it out slowly. "According to my reading of Kirk's logs, the original *Enterprise* had no problem with this level of fear. That crew's fears came only from the ways the creatures looked."

Picard glanced around the bridge. "Yet everyone on

our ship seems to have fallen prey to these overpowering emotions. Most of have not seen the imagery on the screen."

"A weapon," Worf said. "It is a weapon."

Picard nodded. "I agree. They are using some sort of device now. It is—" Picard took a breath as a wave of shuddering ran through him. Riker's eyes grew wide. Picard bit his lower lip and forced the shuddering to stop.

"It is," he began again, "only logical. We defeated them before. They would come back stronger, using the knowledge they gained about us the first time to fight us now."

Riker nodded. "Just as we are doing against them."

Picard nodded. "Number One, with this in mind, I want you to go to engineering. Several of La Forge's people were overwhelmed by the first wave. I am certain he needs assistance. Provide him with some, and make certain that the entire staff is working on a way to shield us from the Furies' power, whatever this is. Do it as quickly as you can, Number One."

"Aye, sir." Riker actually looked relieved to have something to do. He pushed himself out of his chair as though anxious to be away from Picard, and hurried to the turbolift. As he passed Ensign Iket, Riker paused, spoke softly, and then continued on his way. Even in the middle of his own fear, Riker had comfort to spare for others.

Picard was lucky that Riker had turned down his own command. At moments like this, Picard needed someone solid to rely on. Fortunately, he also had Data.

"Mr. Data," Picard said, "observations."

Data pushed away from the console. "The Fury is justifiably certain of its own power. Ancient history from many different societies shows that they were able to enslave peoples in this sector for thousands of years. Earth, Vulcan, and Klingon cultures all show records of their influence or domination."

Picard nodded. "Go on."

Data looked puzzled for a moment before he continued. "It seemed to me, however, that the captain of the Fury vessel did not anticipate your response to its message. Your offer to negotiate confused it, and your mention of diplomats made it pause for a moment."

"In consideration?" Picard asked. He had been so involved in controlling his emotions that he wasn't able to read the emotions in the Fury captain.

"No, sir. If I had to speculate, I would say that it was not familiar with the term. I do not believe that the Furies have negotiated in their recent history. I doubt they even understood what Captain Kirk was trying to do their first time here. The records show that Kirk delayed the battle and was able to talk to them only because they were looking for proof that this area was their home area. Once they found that proof, they attacked."

Picard steepled his fingers and tapped them against his chin. "Speculate more for me, Mr. Data. If they aren't here to negotiate, why did they arrive with only five ships?"

"There could be several explanations, Captain. If your hypothesis is correct and they have developed a device to incapacitate us with fear, five ships might be all they think they need. It would seem, though, based on historic precedent and standard military tactics, that these five ships are an advance point. Scout ships, for lack of a better way of putting it."

Picard felt himself shudder, but he hoped it didn't show.

Data went on. "With that in mind, I looked at strategy. Those five ships appear to be guarding the Furies' entry point. We think the point is a kind of wormhole, but nearly eighty years of observation have shown us that it is not available to our ships, the way the wormhole near Bajor is. However, this wormhole seems to open at the whim of the Furies. Either they have knowledge of when it will open or the wormhole is artificially created."

Data's analysis was calming Picard. It was good to hear someone speaking rationally.

"What do you believe?"

"The evidence points to an artificial creation," Data said. "If the Furies had to time their arrival in the Alpha Quadrant with the opening of the wormhole, they would have sent in their entire invasion force. If these five ships are indeed an advance team, then the hole is artificially created, and we will see other ships arrive through the wormhole shortly."

Picard swallowed. More Furies. It made sense. But it didn't give them much time.

"Sir," Data said. "While you were speaking with the Fury, I took the liberty of running several tests. I hoped to find a source for the emotional distress the Furies' visage seems to cause the crew."

Relief flooded through Picard. "Good thinking."

"Unfortunately, I was unable to find any obvious cause of the distress. The communication seemed like a straightforward intership exchange. The Fury ships were not using any weaponry that our systems can detect."

But that didn't mean the weapons weren't there. For decades, the Federation could not detect a cloaked Romulan warbird even if the bird were within hailing distance.

"I also ran several experiments on this sector of space, thinking perhaps we had run into some sort of field that generated unease within the crew."

Picard felt startled. He hadn't thought of that, even though it was obvious. Too much of his energy was focused on remaining calm.

"And?" he asked.

"Nothing, sir. We seem to be in a normal sector of space."

For some reason, the news did not discourage Picard. It made him realize that there were answers, and answers beyond the Furies' control of the subconscious.

The key was to find those answers before the Furies' attack began in earnest.

"Excellent, Mr. Data," Picard said. "Keep working along those lines. If you need additional resources, let me know."

"Aye, sir." Data turned back to his console.

Picard resisted the urge to cross his fingers. If they could find a way to block the fear the Furies caused, they would have half the battle won. Perhaps more than that. The fact that Data had come up with ideas Picard had not thought of disturbed Picard, and showed, only too clearly, the advantage that fear gave the Furies.

Picard needed to take that advantage away.

And he needed to do it soon.

Chapter Ten

RIKER KEPT HIS HEAD DOWN as he moved through the ship. He had tried, when he first got on the turbolift, to pretend nothing was wrong, but he couldn't. Seeing fear in the other crew members made fear increase within him. And he needed to bring the fear down. Captain Picard felt the same terror, yet he seemed to continually face it. Somehow it weakened Riker's defenses, made him seem less than he was.

He finally understood how the Klingons felt disgraced in battle with the Furies. Riker had survived on a Klingon ship, against the betrayal, the constant danger, the tests made on his human capabilities, and he had seen that as a challenge. Nothing had brought this kind of deep emotion out in him before.

The same things had probably happened to the Klingons in that first fight. They were used to being tough. They knew how to master difficult circumstances. They never suffered from unreasonable fears. Every fear they faced, and faced down, was justified.

A Klingon always weighed the risks and entered into battle knowing the odds. But that time a Klingon general had panicked and turned to the Federation for help. No wonder they never talked about that battle, even in legends.

Now Riker didn't even know what he was fighting. He suspected he was fighting himself.

Throughout the ship, crew members were down. Some had passed out. Others were moaning. A few were running as if the hounds of hell were behind them—and perhaps they were.

An even larger number of crew were getting back on their feet, surveying their surroundings, mastering their feelings, and helping those around them. Their eyes had a haunted look that probably mirrored the look in Riker's eyes. He knew if he survived this he would never again view his own capabilities the same way.

So, coming into engineering seemed like walking into a haven. Three crew members were unconscious, and someone had propped them near the door. Pale, shaking engineers were examining the warp core. Two ensigns were repairing a sensor pad on top of the screen grid.

Geordi was milling through all of it, appearing busy and concerned. The only thing that gave away his own terror was the speed with which he moved. Geordi always hurried when he felt he could do nothing else. He was hurrying now.

The surprise was Redbay. Someone else had made

out the duty rosters this week, and they had placed Redbay in engineering. He now leaned over a console, his forehead propped against the plastic edge of a screen, his lanky frame hunched forward.

"Sam," Riker said.

Redbay snapped to attention, something he never usually did. Redbay's normal movements were languorous, even in battle. He always moved as if he couldn't be bothered, as if the latest threat were a mere inconvenience. This time was different. This time, he gripped the laser pen in one hand and nodded at Riker.

Redbay's eyes were haunted too.

Their gazes met. Two old friends who knew, without saying, what the other had been through.

"The captain sent me down here. He thinks we can block these waves of emotion."

"I do too," Geordi said from behind him, words clipped and businesslike. "I think there's a link between the fear we felt on the station, and the fear felt shipwide here. Most people paralyzed by terror on the *Enterprise* hadn't seen the Fury. And a significant number aren't human and don't have the same subconscious fears. If I were making a hypothesis, I would say that only select Terrans would be frightened by the imagery we saw on the station, yet it affected me. My parents were in Starfleet, and I didn't hear about the more colorful versions of hell until we studied the Furies at the Academy."

"We can rule out smell," Redbay said. "Our noses aren't detecting anything, and the computer says that nothing has changed in the chemical component of the air."

"I don't want to rule anything out yet," Riker said. "Some gases are odorless, and we can still suffer their effects."

"But the computer should be able to read them."

Riker shook his head. "Our systems are good, but they're not perfect. The Furies are clearly sending something our way, and our sensors aren't picking up a beam or a weapon or anything. They've been in this quadrant before, eighty years ago. They've had plenty of time to develop a weapon that will affect us, but one that we can't detect."

"It would help," Geordi said, "if we could determine the nature of the weapon."

"If there is a weapon," Riker said. But he knew he was being too careful. The *Enterprise* had been attacked, he knew that for certain.

"There is," Redbay said. "There has to be."

Riker grinned at his friend. There had to be not because it was logical, but so that they could save face, within themselves. One of the major tests for Academy admission was the ability to subdue fear. A cadet had to be able to face any situation with strength. That way he could negotiate with creatures that terrified him, or keep a cool head in the middle of an attack.

As the captain had.

As Riker attempted to do, and had, if he were being honest with himself. It just hadn't *felt* that way.

It still didn't. His greatest fear was that he would lose control of himself.

He shoved the fear aside.

"I have some ideas, Will," Redbay said. "I've been

thinking about them since"—he paused, grinned, and shrugged—"well, since I got my brain back. Let's assume that the Furies have developed some sort of weapon that does this to us. If so, it must be something that can be projected across distances. To send a gas through a vacuum would require some kind of containment field, and that would be very difficult to hide."

"We don't know the limits of their technology," Geordi said. "They might be able to hide such a field from us."

"Perhaps," Redbay said. "The reactions you had on the station argue for some sort of assault on the senses. Smell is the most logical. But Lieutenant, we were all hit with this wave, as Will calls it, at the same time. You were in a Jeffries tube. One of the ensigns still out cold over there was in the containment field around the warp core."

"And it has a separate air-filtration system," Geordi said.

"So does the Jeffries tube," Riker said, beginning to follow Redbay's argument. "Anything airborne would have taken longer to hit people in these separate areas, and it seemed that we all got hit at once."

"So we can fairly safely rule out smell," La Forge said.

Riker nodded.

"Sound could have reached all of us at the same time," Redbay said, "but unless I miss my guess, Captain Picard was not broadcasting his talk with the Fury shipwide."

"No, he wasn't," Riker said. He frowned. "For the

Furies to be using sound, they would have to broadcast on some sort of wavelength that was carried along on the transmission. And when the conversation was cut the effect should have stopped."

"True," Geordi said. "It would either have to piggyback on the communication with the captain or it would have to travel long distances and somehow pierce the hull and affect all of us at the same time. Again, a containment field would be needed."

"Not likely," Redbay said, "at least not without detection. I was modulating the screens when that first attack hit. I should have noticed something."

"Data was actually monitoring the Furies' vessels," Riker said, "and he found nothing."

"So they are using something subtler, something not quite as obvious, and something that can affect all of us at exactly the same time."

"It would need to be a beam of some kind, but of a kind we don't recognize right off." Geordi's voice was rising with his excitement. "We would have to test for everything."

"Not everything." Riker believed he knew where Redbay was going. "Only physical things, things which would induce an involuntary fear reaction."

"Smell, sound, sight, what else?" Geordi asked.

"No," Redbay said. "Maybe just the reaction to sight, smell, and sound. What does the body produce in reaction to those outside stimuli? Pheromones? I'm not real strong in that area."

"But doesn't that fall under smell?" Riker asked. He didn't know either. But he knew who to ask.

Geordi shrugged. "It's outside my area of expertise,

too. I suggest we consult with Dr. Crusher. I also think we might want to test you, me, and Data to see if we brought anything back from the station. Maybe the Furies baited a trap for us, lured us over there, and had us bring back the trigger. The trigger might be some sort of virus, airborne, and then they pull the switch on their ship, and voilà, we all get scared."

"It's one theory," Redbay said.

Riker agreed. His logical mind said there needed to be a reason why the Furies did what they did on the Brundage Station. They couldn't have done such a thing just in spite.

"Follow that idea, too," Riker said. "The captain did say that the Furies would be stronger this time."

"Did the first run-in with them have this weapon?" Redbay asked.

"Not that the records show," Riker said. "The reaction back then seemed to be more out of fear of what they looked like, what they represented. Kirk and the rest of that crew never mention that the Furies used such fear as a weapon."

"Except," Geordi said slowly, "those old reports were of cultural demons and devils, figures of myth returned. The Klingons put a high store in that sort of thing, even now. It caused their extreme reaction, that ended up bringing in the original *Enterprise*. Remember Worf's reaction when Kahless returned?"

Riker nodded.

"This is different," Geordi went on. "When I got hit in the Jeffries tube, I was flashing back on that fire when I was five. I could have sworn everything on the ship was burning up."

Redbay nodded. "I was back reliving the horror of the day my parents died."

And Riker, who had never allowed himself real terror, hadn't had anything to pin his fear on. Somehow that bothered him even more. "What's your point, Geordi?" he asked, wanting to move his own thinking away from the terror and his ability or lack of ability to control it.

"This fear hit us, and instead of finding an external cause, our minds searched for the last time we had felt this kind of terror and made up the rest. This wasn't cultural. This is sophisticated."

"A weapon," Redbay agreed. "We're back to that again. But a weapon that somehow triggers fear reactions normally caused by sights, smells, and sounds."

Geordi grinned. "If it's a weapon, we can find it. And we can block it."

Riker grinned too. Even though the fear was still present, like the hum of a machine in the background, it suddenly became tolerable. "Then we need to find a systematic way of searching for it."

"Yes," Redbay started.

Then Picard's voice cut over the comm system. "Senior staff to the conference room."

The order made Riker shudder. He didn't want to know what emergency had broken now.

But that was his fear talking.

He took a deep breath. Geordi clapped him on the shoulder and turned to Redbay. "Lieutenant," Geordi said, "go ahead and begin a search. I'll be back as soon as I can."

Redbay nodded and bent over the consoles. Riker and Geordi left engineering at full run.

"Sam's creative," Riker said as they got on the turbolift. "If anyone can find out what's going on, Sam can."

"I hope so," Geordi said. "Because I have the feeling we don't have a lot of time."

Chapter Eleven

BEVERLY CRUSHER STOPPED outside the door to Deanna Troi's quarters. Fear made her heart race, and because she wasn't sure if the fear was entirely real or a product of her fevered imagination, she actually knocked.

And received no response.

"What am I doing?" she whispered. Around her the corridor was filled with dazed crew members. At an intersection a short distance away a crew member lay unconscious, her arms covering her face as if something had been hitting her when she passed out.

Beverly hesitated, wanting to go to the woman, then forced her mind back on her goal. She took a deep breath, brushed aside a strand of loose red hair, and then said, "Computer, emergency medical override."

The door hissed open, and there was Deanna on the

floor, her face pressed against the carpet, one hand raised and the other bent awkwardly beneath her.

It looked as if she'd been trying to crawl to the door to escape something terrible behind her.

Beverly's fears had been real.

She knelt beside Deanna, and as she pulled out her medical tricorder, she smoothed Deanna's hair away from her face. Deanna's eyes were rolled back in their sockets, lashes fluttered. Her mouth was partially open, and her skin was clammy.

Beverly flipped open the tricorder and ran it over Deanna. Her pulse was too rapid, her blood pressure was high, and the levels of adrenaline in her system were off the charts. Yet she wasn't moving. These readings matched the readings from Lieutenant Young, and the result appeared to be the same:

Deanna was dying.

Beverly grabbed a needle from her kit, and then paused. To wake Deanna would be to put her through hell. According to the tricorder readings, Deanna was still conscious, but her system was overloaded. To stimulate her, to make her mind deal with all of the input it was getting, would probably push her over the edge into total insanity.

No. A sedative would be better, and something to block the psychic transfers. There were a number of drugs that would do the trick. The problem was that they were all in sickbay.

"Computer," Beverly said, "download all information on Betazoid empathic powers and blocks into my sickbay computers."

"Download complete."

"Step one," Beverly said to herself. She found the

99

sedative she was looking for in her bag, and gave it to Deanna. Deanna's eyes slowly closed and she seemed to breathe a little smoother.

"Computer, is anyone in the transporter rooms?"

"The transporter rooms are empty."

Just what she needed. Beverly bit back a retort.

"Find Transporter Chief Anderson."

"Transporter Chief Anderson is in engineering."

Beverly hit her comm badge. "Anderson," she said. "This is Dr. Crusher. I need an emergency beam-across to sickbay."

"I'm sorry, Doctor," Anderson said. "Someone accidentally blasted the transporter controls here. Have you checked with the transporter rooms?"

"Yes, I have, Chief, and no one is in any of them."

"I could go—"

"Do so, and if I'm not in sickbay when you get to the transporter room, beam me directly there."

"Aye, sir."

Beverly slung her kit over her left shoulder, then picked up Deanna, one arm under her back and the other under her knees. Beverly staggered forward for a moment, then straightened her back, letting Deanna's weight settle more firmly in her arms.

"I can do this," she said to herself. "Just one step at a time and I'll make it."

Slowly, she headed for the door, and by the time she was outside Deanna's quarters she was gaining confidence. And speed. It had been a long time since she had carried dead weight for some distance. Certainly not since she had been on the *Enterprise.*

But she could do it. The key was to breathe deeply and move at a constant pace.

Then Captain Picard's voice echoed through the small corridor. "Senior officers to the conference room."

"Excellent timing, Jean-Luc," Beverly muttered.

Lieutenant Worf was the last to arrive in the conference room. He had stopped by his quarters to touch the *bat'leth* that Kahless had given him, a sign to Worf of his own courage.

He was appalled at his initial reaction to the Furies. He had studied the Klingon response to the original Fury attack all those years ago, and had thought it impossible for a modern Klingon to act in a panicked way.

Then he had argued with the captain about the value of fear.

Argued.

As if he needed to justify his own fears.

Cowards justified their fears.

And Worf was no coward.

He strode into the conference room as if nothing were wrong. Riker and La Forge had entered just before him. As Worf suspected, he had lost no time in stopping at his quarters.

In fact, he had probably gained them all time. He had to remind himself of Klingon honor, not Klingon shame.

Captain Picard was standing beside his chair. The others were sitting. But two chairs were empty.

Dr. Crusher's chair, and Counselor Troi's.

Deanna's empty chair seemed to scream at him, call him a fool and a coward all at once.

Worf glanced at the door. He should have thought

of the effect this overwhelming emotion would have had on Deanna. The fear had caught them all off guard. Deanna would have handled things well if she had been prepared, but she hadn't. None of them had.

Riker was also staring at the empty chair. He must have forgotten, also. That thought gave Worf no comfort.

As a unit, both men started for the door.

"I called a meeting, gentlemen," Picard said softly.

"But Deanna—" Worf said.

Picard nodded once. He understood too. "She will be here if she can."

"But shouldn't someone check on her?" Riker asked.

"Sickbay informs me that Dr. Crusher has already done so." The captain clasped his hands behind his back. Worf recognized the gesture. The captain would say no more. But he just couldn't let it go at that.

"Begging the captain's pardon," Worf said, "but I believe we should check on her condition."

"I understand your concern, Lieutenant, but Dr. Crusher will see to Deanna's needs. Right now, I require your presence here."

Worf took a deep breath. He knew his duty. But he also knew how valuable Deanna was to the ship.

And to him.

He turned and came back to his chair, sitting heavily. Commander Riker was still by the door, looking indecisive. He never looked that indecisive.

"You too, Will," Picard said softly. "We're all concerned for Deanna, but I'm afraid that right now we have other matters to attend to. I just received a scrambled communication from Admiral Kirschbaum. The *Starships Madison* and *Idaho*—"

The door hissed open and Beverly Crusher hurried in. Her long red hair was plastered to her face, and a line of sweat ran down the side of her uniform.

"Forgive me for being late, Captain," she said, and slumped into the nearest chair.

The terror Worf had been feeling all day rose. He had to clench his massive fists to contain it. "The counselor?" he asked.

Dr. Crusher glanced at him, her mouth a thin line. "I don't know, Worf. I got her to sickbay, and put her under sedation. I also used some blockers, hoping to stop the empathic response. But when I found her, her system was overloading."

"Like Lieutenant Young's?" Riker asked.

"It's similar," Dr. Crusher said, "but not the same. The terror we've all been feeling has amplified in Deanna. I don't believe she saw anything or did anything to trigger this. She calmed noticeably once we administered the block."

"Do you believe that she'll be conscious any time soon?" the captain asked.

"I don't know if it's a good idea for us to let her to be conscious until we settle this," Dr. Crusher said. "I'm not sure how much she can take."

"It is only going to get worse," Worf said. "We have not yet faced the Furies directly. We have only contacted them from a distance."

"Do you expect us to face them directly, Mr. Worf?" the captain asked.

"I believe, Captain, given what we found on

Brundage Station, and given the past history of the Furies, that we will face them directly in a fight."

"If they board the ship or come into contact directly with Deanna," Dr. Crusher said, "I cannot vouch for her sanity. In fact, I can't vouch for any of our sanity. I had hoped to get her help with Lieutenant Young, since he was the first. I believe all of his trouble is psychological, not physical."

"Hmm," the captain said, obviously seeing the implications in what Dr. Crusher was saying.

Worf agreed with the doctor. He had thought he might be immune, yet he had felt the terror of the Furies. He had thought he would react differently from his ancestors. But he hadn't. He had been just as terrified from the contact.

The key, though, as the captain had pointed out, was to overcome that fear.

And he would, for his own sake as well as Deanna's.

"Well," the captain said, "we must leave Deanna and Lieutenant Young in your capable care, Beverly."

He unclasped his hands, then clasped them as if he didn't know what to do with them. "Admiral Kirschbaum contacted me again. The *Starships Madison* and *Idaho* will arrive in three hours. The Klingons and Vulcans will assist us as well. Two of the Klingons' closest Birds-of-Prey will be here at the same time as the starships. The Vulcan ship *T'Pau* will arrive within four hours."

"Only two ships?" Worf asked. The fear he had been trying to suppress rose again. The Klingons would not shame themselves. Not again.

"I am told, Mr. Worf, that the Klingon Homeworld

is massing two lines of defense. One is here, and the other, the main one, is farther inside the border to Klingon space. The Federation is doing the same. We are simply the front line, the first battle of what may turn out to be a very long and costly war."

It was uncharacteristic of Klingons to have a back-up line of defense. Worf crossed his arms and leaned back, forcing himself into silence. His people had acted so impulsively during the first encounter with the Furies, it made sense for them to act more conservatively this time.

"So no one believes we'll survive this," Commander Riker said without a trace of bitterness.

"Starfleet is operating under the assumptions posited by Captain Kirk, Number One. The first *Enterprise* barely managed to beat one Fury ship. Granted, it was a very different ship from the five we are facing out there, but the thought is that the Furies will arrive stronger this time. Five ships would tend to back up that line of thinking."

"We're stronger now, too," Geordi said.

"We are, Mr. La Forge, and we have to hope that the Furies do not know that. But we cannot rely on their ignorance as a source of defense. Starfleet has had a Furies scenario for eighty years. The first ship on the scene is to negotiate with the Furies, and should that fail, the ship is to consider a breach of the Furies Point an act of war."

"But they attacked the Brundage Station," Worf said.

Picard nodded. "With the Furies' attack on the station, the wartime analysis is assured. We are to do our best to defeat them here, but Starfleet believes that the Furies will sweep through our defenses and move into the quadrant. Hence the backup forces, both on our side and on the Klingon side."

"They could give us a chance before they give up on us," Geordi mumbled.

Worf agreed, but said nothing. Sometimes it was the place of a warrior to die, and to do so on the front lines of battle would be a great honor.

"They have not given up on us, Mr. La Forge," the captain said. "If they had, they would not be sending so many ships here. But we learned in our first encounter with the Furies to be careful. We are not facing another space-traveling race with equal or lesser powers. Instead we are facing a race that ruled this entire quadrant for possibly over two millennia and want to do so again. We must respond accordingly."

Worf moved forward slightly. "What other forces will join in the larger battle?"

"We don't know." The captain took a deep breath, as if he had been hesitating about sharing this next information. "The Romulans have refused to come to our aid. The Cardassians have decided to wait until they know the outcome of this first battle. They claim their concerns are not simply for this sector of space, but for the quadrant itself."

Riker snorted, but said nothing.

"And the wormhole near *Deep Space Nine*. Have the people there been warned?" La Forge asked.

"The entire quadrant now knows and is preparing at this point. Admiral Kirschbaum hopes to have more support as time goes on. Some planets simply do not have strong defensive capabilities. It is up to us to make certain, if possible, that the Furies do not go beyond this area."

Worf found himself nodding in agreement. The most important fight was here. The Federation and the Empire would lose the advantage if the fight spread out over the neighboring star systems and into the quadrant.

"That presents a problem, Captain," Dr. Crusher said. "Even with this limited contact, the crew is not responding well. I have twenty-seven people in sick-bay under heavy sedation. Those who can function are picking up the slack and encouraging those who are marginal. But our biggest problem is with the families. We are managing, but certainly we aren't performing anywhere near capacity. I don't know how many personnel would be able to hold their posts during an attack."

The captain smiled tightly. "I am aware of that, Doctor. It is ourselves and our reactions that we must conquer first before moving on to the Furies. To that end, Mr. La Forge, what have you discovered in engineering?"

"Nothing yet, sir," Geordi said, "but we are working on several theories. Lieutenant Redbay believes that this fear response is artificially created and carried on a beam of some sort. In theory I agree with him. He's working right now to discover the source of the reaction and to see if he can block it."

"How long do you estimate this will take?" the captain asked.

Geordi shook his head. "I wish I could tell you, Captain. But right now, we're working on supposition and logic. No definitive proof at all. And since we don't know what we're looking for, we don't know how to block it or what it will take to do so."

"Lieutenant Redbay's supposition would seem to be a correct one," Data said. "The fear response in this ship is, according to my analysis of the old records, far stronger than the reaction the original *Enterprise* crew had. It also does not follow the same pattern that theirs did."

Picard nodded. "Well, if we cannot block the attack from without, we must stop it from within."

Worf knew of the battle within. Klingons fought it most of their lives. "Klingons have a technique called KloqPoq that might serve us well."

"I'm not sure this is the time, Mr. Worf," Riker said.

"KloqPoq does not always entail a ritual," Worf said. "The shortened version requires only the touch of oil upon the forehead combined with words of strength." There had been many times over the years that he had used the ritual, and it had worked every time to calm him.

"Right now," the captain said, "I am willing to try anything that will help the crew. Number One, I want you to issue a statement to the crew about cultural rituals such as the one Mr. Worf described. Some of these might have been invented in response to prehistoric contact with the Furies. We cannot rule any of these rituals out. But do stress, Number One, that these rituals cannot take time away from duty. The shorter the better."

Picard turned and looked at him. "Mr. Worf, you

may perform the short version on any crew member who desires it."

Worf nodded. "Thank you, sir." He was pleased that the captain allowed him to help.

"In the meantime, Dr. Crusher, is there any physical way to block the fear response?"

She frowned and pushed a strand of red hair aside, smearing the dirt and sweat coating her forehead. "There are several in humans, Captain, but I wouldn't want to use any of these before a battle. They also inhibit other responses as well."

"Is there any way to isolate the fear response and block only it?"

"I have several theories," she said, "but I have had no time to focus on them."

"How long would it take to bring one of your theories to fruition?"

"Give me an hour."

The captain nodded. "Then make it so, Beverly. Blocking our own fears would be the best line of defense against this first attack by the Furies."

"I agree," she said.

The captain turned from her to face all his officers. His decisive movements led Worf to believe that the captain had a plan. Whether he did or not was immaterial. The fact that he *acted* as if he did mattered most. It engendered hope in the officers, which would then inspire the crew.

"There is one more potential problem," the captain said. "While we might assume that these five ships are the only ships we will face, we cannot believe that assumption. These ships might be the advance guard for an invasion force. If that is the case, the Starfleet vessels, the Klingon Birds-of-Prey, and the *T'Pau* will not be enough to keep the force from sweeping into the quadrant."

A chill ran through Worf. "Have you evidence of this, Captain?"

"It is only a theory at this point, Mr. Worf."

"I believe this theory to be accurate," Data said. "The evidence suggests that the five ships are waiting for something. Most likely a second, larger force."

Worf nodded. That would be simply good tactics. A small advance force before risking a larger one.

Picard focused his intense gaze on all of them, and Worf straightened his shoulders.

"I do not want an invasion force to come through that wormhole," Picard said, his voice firm. "In fact, I do not want any more Fury ships to come into this quadrant. Therefore, in addition to finding ways to prevent the Furies from attacking us, we must find a way to close the wormhole."

The silence in the room was palpable.

Until now, it seemed, no one had really thought about what all-out war with the Furies would mean. But the thought of an invasion force seemed suddenly very real to Worf. These ships needed to be stopped now and the wormhole closed. Worf understood and he felt ready for the fight.

The captain walked around the table and stopped behind Data. "Mr. Data, I want you to make that wormhole your primary source of study. I need to know the most effective method to close it. And I need it fast."

"Aye, sir," Data said.

The captain made eye contact with each of his officers. When his gaze rested on Worf, Worf nodded back. The captain's confidence was restoring Worf's confidence. He could feel it giving him strength as each minute went by.

"I don't think I need to impress upon you all the importance of what we do here," the captain said. "We are the Federation's flagship, and I have never worked with a stronger, more capable crew in my entire career. The *Enterprise* defeated the Furies once. She shall do so again."

And somehow, for that moment in time, Worf believed that what the captain said was true.

Chapter Twelve

THE SHIP WAS GROWING COLD, the air thin, and the food scarce. Some minor functionary was not doing his job.

Again.

Vergo Vedil unfolded his body from the command chair and groaned as he did so. The bridge of the *Erinyes* had been designed by Ak'lins. Web-footed and secure, they had never thought that a leader might be a Zebub. He had to struggle to keep his hoofed feet from sliding out from underneath him.

It was not dignified for the Vergo of the *Erinyes* to slip and fall on his spiny backside. He scratched behind one of his horns, nearly breaking a nail, and then sucked at the air, catching sweetmeats in the thin strands of saliva that coated his mouth. He glanced around and could almost see the entire distance across the bridge. The atmosphere was far too thin. In a moment he would see that fixed, and someone would pay for the oversight.

He slowly stretched his muscles. This bout of waiting seemed interminable. He had thought the advance guard would have all the pleasure of the invasion. He had not realized that the hours between his first attack and the arrival of the fleet would be long, and filled with emptiness.

Ythion had argued against keeping the live one, and Vedil had had too much fun killing the others. The presents he left for the Unclean should have frightened them beyond their capacity for reason. And if they had had their souls with them, he would have scattered them to air, cutting them open.

He lightly brushed the doll likeness of himself hanging on his side. It felt thick and full, as his life had been to this point. His soul was safe, but it reassured him to check it at times.

He faced the front viewscreen and stared at the Unclean ship hanging in space. They had contacted him again. Perhaps his approach had been too narrow. He had used what the Unclean captive had thought of as a Terran attack. He should have noted that a sweep of the Unclean's mind informed him that many races from heaven filled the ships now. Perhaps Vedil should have allowed one of the Sakill, with their ridged foreheads and long braided hair, to accompany him. Or even a Jequat, a one-eyed stone giant, to squint at the puny captain of the Unclean.

That would have silenced him forever.

The Unclean ship had not attacked yet. Perhaps it never would. Perhaps he would remain, guardian of the Entrance to Heaven, leader of a battle that would never occur.

"Vergo, they have received another transmission." His first assistant bowed before him, the snakes in her hair floating around her, their mouths opening and closing in the ever-thinning air.

He scooped a maggot from his cheek, watched the creature climb in the curve of his longest nail, and then scraped the nail against his left fang. The maggot was sweet and juicy, cool against his tongue.

The rest of his staff watched him, knowing that when he ate so obviously in front of them he was breaking etiquette and showing his displeasure. Hands, claws, and flippers rested against controls, waiting for his next command, or his next outburst.

"And of course we know, Dea, what that transmission said." He swiveled his head until the tip of one horn brushed against the nearest snake.

She jumped away as if burned. "No, Vergo, but we are working on it."

"Working on it. Such an old-fashioned, out-of-date term. These communications are not sophisticated. We have their ancient codes from the ship of Kirk. We should be able to understand what they are saying."

She swallowed, and all the snakes floating about her head closed their mouths, as if in sympathy. "Yes, Vergo."

"I am glad we understand each other," he said, and used his horn to decapitate the snake he had been toying with. Green goo billowed in the atmosphere along with tiny bugs, half a dozen or more. He sucked them in through his teeth.

She blinked in obvious pain. "I will do better, Vergo."

"You will have to," he said. "Since I am now removing your badge of power. You shall go to the food tanks below, see what is thinning the air, and double the level of edibles in the atmosphere."

She nodded. The snakes all watched him, as wary as she was. "Below, then, Vergo." She pivoted on one small, Unclean-like foot, and crossed the bridge. As she stepped into the mobile stairs, the snakes on her head dove at the single snake carcass. They ripped and shredded it in their haste to devour the remains.

Much like his people when they sensed weakness.

"B'el," Vedil said. "You shall monitor the Unclean ship."

B'el bobbed the center of his three heads. The others were already too busy watching the screens. "Vergo," said the first head, "the Unclean are trying to communicate with us again."

Vedil snorted. "Do these creatures do nothing other than talk?"

This was the third attempt at communication. It disturbed him. After their discovery of the outpost and its dead crew, and especially after his first transmission, this Unclean ship should have been his.

"O'pZ," he said to the Ak'lin at the science console. "Has our beam shut off?"

"No, Veeerrrgo." Her beaklike mouth often got stuck on sibilants. He had almost given her a position where she need not talk in the heat of battle. But Ak'lins had a gift for engineering, architecture, and science. O'pZ was the most talented scientist he knew.

115

And therefore extremely valuable.

"What evidence have you of the beam's effect?"

She lowered her scaly head and hunched her ridged back forward, as if protecting her soft underbelly. "None, Vergo. It is as if the beam is having no effect."

"We should destroy the Unclean ship," her lover, Prote, said. His useless wings unfurled at the thought, nearly hitting B'el.

"And if we do that, we lose all the precious knowledge they hold in their minds and in their electronic systems." Vedil steadied himself against his chair. His feet slid against the slick floor, and he had to struggle for a moment to keep his balance.

He glanced around, then decided. "Increase the beam's intensity. We have ten hours to conquer them without destroying their ship. I would prefer to give this vessel to the fleet as a prize when they come through, rather than have them fly through a ring of debris."

"Vergo, the debris from one puny vessel will not make a difference to two hundred of our ships," Prote said.

Vedil lowered his gaze and glared at Prote. "And the loss of one navigation officer will not make a difference in our return to heaven."

Prote's wings curled and he bowed his head. "Yes, Vergo."

"I thought the beam would work quicker than it has," the Ak'lin said. "I thought it would be easier to enslave them."

"It will be easy to enslave them," Vedil said. "You forget the ease with which we captured their outpost.

Once they see us face-to-face, they will be unable to resist our dominance."

He grinned at his crew. They watched him warily.

"We shall toy with the Unclean for another hour or so, and then we shall make them ours. But I would like to remind them how powerless they are against us, and an hour or two of futile struggle is all we need."

"When the fleet comes through, the Unclean will know we are conquerors," Prote said, obviously trying to make up for his earlier mistakes.

"They will know it before the fleet comes through," Vedil said. "By the time the fleet joins us, this tiny Unclean vessel shall lead us into the promised land, its crew eager to share its enslavement with its companions in the stars beyond."

Chapter Thirteen

REDBAY FOCUSED on the screens in front of him. If he concentrated on work, his fears—the memories of that horrid year when he lost his family and scavenged through the remains of Nyo colony alone—didn't overwhelm him. Sometimes they caught him in the throat or the gut. Sometimes he felt shivers running through him, and once he thought of asking Ensign Moest for a hug. Well, not really. She was beautiful, and he wouldn't mind a bit of female comfort at the moment, but he had learned his lesson early: never start a shipboard romance. If the thing went sour, there was nowhere to hide.

He grinned to himself. Thinking about women was a lot easier than thinking about the past.

But he needed to focus on the task at hand. The

quicker they blocked whatever the Furies were doing to them, the better things would get.

Or so he kept telling himself.

He was doing tests on types of subspace carrier waves, hoping to stumble on something. To him, subspace or interspace seemed the only two logical ways the Furies could send some sort of fear trigger. If the captain's supposition was right, the Furies had the capability to form wormholes. They clearly understood more about the physics of subspace and interspace than the Federation did.

The tests appeared as multicolored light on his screens. Those light patterns sent shivers through him. Multicolored light used to send him screaming from his safe room for years after his parents died. The Federation investigated the deaths on Nyo, but never found evidence of the light creatures. Some counselors believed that Redbay had made them up to cope with the trauma. Those counselors believed that everyone had died of disease or some undetectable cause.

Not genocide.

But he hadn't made it up. His memories were still clear. He had seen those creatures and he had hidden from them, and he had been the sole survivor.

But he was here now. On the *Enterprise*.

Looking at multicolored light patterns *he* had made.

And then he squinted. The effort it took him to block his fears delayed his own understanding of the pink cone he saw on the screen before him.

"Geordi," he said, his voice shaking with awe. "I found it."

119

La Forge left his seat and hurried to Redbay's side, leaning over his shoulder.

"Look. Right here."

Redbay put a finger on the screen. In his search, he had changed the look of the screen to a variety of different computer models. This one looked like a two-dimensional representation used long before computer imaging came into play. He had only called it up after exhausting the other options.

On it, the Furies' ships showed up as black dots near the yellow, glowing Furies Point. Brundage Station was another black square with a bit of silver light trickling off it, as if it had been raining in space, and now the rain was dripping dry. He had his theories about that, but they weren't important just yet. What was important were the multicolored light waves that ran across the screen, representing the *Enterprise*'s search for the source of the fear.

And, as the light passed over the main Fury ship, a cone of pink light appeared, enveloping the *Enterprise.*

"Wow," La Forge said when the cone became visible. "Can you freeze that? Can we study it as it is?"

Redbay pushed a few buttons. His multicolored light waves disappeared and only the pink cone remained.

"At our position," he said, "the radius of that cone is over a thousand kilometers and it extends beyond our sensor range."

"But what are they projecting?" La Forge asked more to himself than to Redbay. He bent over the nearest panel, running his own checks.

Redbay matched it, fingers shaking. "I don't have a reading yet on the content of that beam, but this is clearly how they're manipulating our emotions. At this frequency in interspace, the beam goes through everything, including our heads."

La Forge glanced at Redbay. A shiver ran down Redbay's spine. The fear rose, as if someone had turned up the volume.

Maybe someone had.

"If they can project something that makes us feel fear," La Forge said softly, "we can block it." Then he paused. "You said interspace?"

Redbay nodded. "That's how they're projecting whatever it is they're projecting. Through interspace."

La Forge paced for a moment, then came back and stood over the cone image. "Interspace. The original *Enterprise* stumbled into interspace during the first meetings with the Tholians? I wonder . . ." La Forge seemed to be talking only to himself.

Redbay suddenly remembered that part of his history class. It had again been the original *Enterprise* and their encounter with the Tholians. But beyond the successful outcome, and the fact that interspace almost took Captain Kirk, he couldn't remember more. But it was clear La Forge did.

La Forge turned to Redbay. "What if the beam they send out is harmless in this universe—but opens a conduit into interspace in the area affected by the beam? Interspace can have a devastating effect on the human nervous system, leading to paranoia and insanity. What if they've managed to control and amplify that effect?"

Redbay grinned. "You might be on to something there. I'll run the checks."

Suddenly, beneath his fear was an elation. La Forge was right. Redbay felt lot better.

He could concentrate now on the task at hand.

"That's it. We've got it," he told La Forge.

La Forge nodded. "I'll tell the captain. I bet this will make his day."

"And Dr. Crusher," Redbay said.

La Forge stopped, and then nodded. "The doctor on the original *Enterprise* came up with something to block the effects, didn't he." He patted Redbay on the shoulder. "On my way."

Redbay turned back to his panel, his fingers flying over the keys. He had work to do, and now he at least knew he was making progress.

She felt as if she were the only physician working on a plague.

Beverly Crusher sighed and ran her fingers through her hair, pushing it back from her forehead. Her eyes were gritty, as if she had gone too long without sleep. She leaned her head against the computer display and gulped the fear down.

Patience, Beverly, she thought. *Take your time.*

Over the years, she had learned that taking her time was the only way to really hurry. Any other method caused her to make mistakes.

She took a sip of the Bajoran root tea that was supposed to calm fears. It was warm and bitter. Then she sat up and peered through the glass of her research area into the sickbay.

Her flu patients were under heavy sedation. They

had awakened earlier, convinced they were dying. She had been unable to calm them; instead she had put them under and hoped that the drug blocked the emotions as well as consciousness. They didn't appear to be having any more bad dreams, so her guess was probably right.

Deanna lay very still on her bed as well. When Beverly had returned to sickbay, she had taken Deanna's pulse just to double-check the machines. Deanna had looked still as death.

Perhaps that was Beverly's fear: losing her friend to an unnecessary cause.

A few other beds were filled with crew members injured in that first wave of fear that swept the station. The medical staff had had a run on the station just after Beverly had left to find Deanna: a series of scrapes, scratches, and burns, all minor—and blown entirely out of proportion because of the fears.

The cases that remained were people brought in by others, people who had been too terrified to notice that they were hurt. Beverly had made a note of their names; when and if they got through this crisis, she wanted Deanna to make a full report on their psychological states.

If Deanna recovered.

Beverly sighed and took another sip of the tea, wincing at its taste.

Then she paused, rolled the tea around on her tongue, and swallowed.

Her tongue was numb. Not completely without sensation, but she had lost enough sensation to get a prickly feeling around the edges.

She had used the root tea before, often on long stressful nights, and had never found that her judgment was impaired.

But it always reduced her stress.

Just like it had calmed her fears now.

She wasn't shaking anymore. She hadn't shaken since she had her first cup.

Then she smiled, pulled out a test tube, and poured the tea in it. The liquid stained the sides of the tube orange. She put the tube in the compositor and had it analyze the contents. While it mixed and remixed the chemicals, Beverly got up and went into sickbay proper. She passed the fear patients and went directly to the flu patients. They were still on the diagnostic beds. She flipped on the overhead screens, and watched as she read the levels.

The flu was running its course. They would be on their feet again in a day or so. But she wasn't interested in their virus. She was interested in brain waves or any indication of REM sleep.

The patients appeared to be sleeping soundly, dreamlessly, and their physical symptoms confirmed it. Heartbeat, respiration, and blood pressure readings had returned to normal—or as near to normal as it was physically possible with the Xotic Flu.

She called up their readings from the past few hours, ever since she had given them the sedative.

No dreams.

None.

The fears were buried, for now.

She went back into her research station. The chemical component of the Bajoran root tea blinked on her screen. As she had thought, the tea had a mild sedative. Very mild, a kind, the computer told her (and her own experience confirmed), that did not impair thoughts or cause drowsiness. It took the edge off certain emotions by blocking the chemical components of those emotions within the body. It did not affect motor skills or judgment.

"Dr. Crusher?" Chief Engineer La Forge's voice came over the comm.

"Go ahead," she said.

"Doctor," La Forge said, "we think the beam hitting us controls and amplifies the effects of interspace."

"Interspace?" She let the word sink in. Why hadn't she thought of that possibility?

"Yes, Doctor," La Forge said.

"Damn," she said softly to herself.

"Excuse me, Doctor?" La Forge said.

"Sorry, Geordi," she said, half laughing. "I'll get right on it. I think I may be able to come up with a block."

"Good," La Forge said. "Out."

She turned her attention back to her screen. With a few keystrokes she had the Theragen formula up on the screen, along with the history of its development and use. For the next few minutes she read, letting the exact details of the drug back into her mind. Its first use was as a nerve gas, developed by the Klingons. But Dr. McCoy on the first *Enterprise* had diluted the drug to stop the effects of interspace on the crew. His diluted form was called the Theragen derivative.

She studied McCoy's work. McCoy had diluted the Theragen with alcohol, but she thought it would make a better mix with the Bajoran tea—that way it would not only block the fear, but have a calming effect on the crew.

125

She asked the computer to confirm that analysis, and the computer did. Replication possible in both liquid and gaseous form.

Beverly smiled. With a lot of help from Geordi, she had come up with a solution much faster than she had expected.

But barely within the captain's deadline.

She hit her comm badge. "Captain?"

"Picard here." His voice sounded firm and steady. She wondered how he managed that when she knew how he felt. The fears sent by the Furies had affected him too.

"I have found a way to help block the fears within the crew."

"Excellent. If you believe it will work, begin treatment immediately."

He was on edge. She could hear it in his tone.

"Captain, I do have to tell you that what I have come up with is partially a mild sedative."

"Sedative?" His voice rose. "Doctor, we may be about to face the most dangerous enemy known to the Federation, and you want to sedate my crew?"

"Yes, sir." She smiled. She had known he would react like that to the word. Better to get it out of the way now. "The sedative will calm the emotions only. It will not affect judgment or impair motor skills. Since I was unable to test it fully, however, I do not know how long its effects will last." She took a deep breath. "I need to also add small quantities of Theragen derivative to the sedative, to help block the effects of interspace."

The captain did not answer immediately. Perhaps

she shouldn't have worried about impaired judgment from the drug. The fear was doing that all by itself. Captain Picard usually made decisions much quicker than this.

"How long will it take you to inoculate the entire crew?"

"I won't have to inoculate them," she said. "I can make this sedative mixed with the Theragen derivative into a gas and flood the air filtration systems. I'll have to let Geordi know so that the systems won't automatically purify it. Other than that, no one will even notice except that their fears will have eased. They won't abate completely, but everyone will be calmer."

"Proceed," Picard said, and signed off.

Beverly took another sip of her root tea and smiled at the mug. Then she turned and punched in the sequence to begin synthesizing the tea and mixing it with Theragen derivative. This just might be the complete answer. She hoped so.

Commander Riker took a deep breath and uncrossed his arms. Somehow, just sitting beside Captain Picard on the bridge calmed him. Everything was calming him. He was regaining control, even without Dr. Crusher's help. When the gas filled the ship, he would be prepared, and maybe feel like his own self again.

On the screen before them, the entire bridge crew was studying Redbay's discovery: the wave of emotion they had all felt was actually sent in the form of a cone-shaped wave that created an interspace conduit.

And the *Enterprise* was stuck in the middle of it. The wave picked up and amplified—or maybe twisted would be a better way of putting it—the adverse effects of interspace on the human mind. The more he studied the data Redbay and La Forge had come up with, the prouder he felt of the crew of the *Enterprise*. They had withstood a very vicious attack and kept their sanity.

"At least we know that our unusual feelings have been manufactured," Picard said.

"That eased the mind of everyone on the engineering staff," Riker said.

"Yes, I can see how it would." Picard stood and tugged on his shirt. "I hope we have as much success in blocking the effects of the wave."

"Lieutenant Redbay believes we will," Riker said. "He and La Forge are researching the incident that occurred with the original *Enterprise*. It should give them some help."

Picard only nodded his agreement.

"Captain," Worf said, "I have received a short, encrypted message from the *Madison*. They will arrive within the hour."

"Did they say anything about the *Idaho*?"

"The ships are traveling in tandem, sir."

Picard nodded. He stared at the screen another moment, frowning at the data about the interspace beam.

"Captain, those ships will fly straight into that beam," Riker said.

"They will encounter it sooner than we did," Data added. "The strength of the cone-shaped beam at its outer edge might be weaker, but the closer they come the more they will feel its effects."

"Without warning," Riker said, "they will go through the same feelings we did."

"I understand that, Number One," Picard said. "I am trying to figure out a way to communicate to them without letting the Furies know that we have ameliorated the effects of their transmission."

"Oh, I know how to do that, sir," Riker said. "Captain Kiser is quite a poker player. I met him on Rigel in a galaxy-wide tournament."

Picard nodded and seemed to take a deep, almost relaxing breath.

Riker suddenly felt as if he wanted to smile. Dr. McCoy's Theragen derivative and Dr. Crusher's sedative gas must be working. The feeling of fear was clearly reduced. It wasn't completely gone, but it was better.

"Kiser and I," Riker said, "were the only humans left in the contest. We worked out a series of signals that allowed us to eliminate the others—"

"You cheated, Number One?"

"Not exactly," Riker said. "It became clear early on that it wasn't a clean tournament, and that the Ferengi sponsors had set up their own people to win. We just . . . how should I say this . . . made sure that wouldn't happen."

"I do not see how a game of chance will enable you to communicate with Captain Kiser," Data said. "It could not carry the needed information."

"It means, Mr. Data, that Commander Riker and Captain Kiser have already developed a method for saying one thing and meaning another," Picard said. "You will need to bury Dr. Crusher's formula for the sedative in the message as well as the theory of the

Furies' fear wave being sent via interspace. The poker signals will only alert him to the fact the information is there."

Data nodded, understanding.

"Yes, sir," Riker said. "I will tell him that this is a view of the Brundage Station and they need to review it immediately. Since they've already seen Brundage Station, Kiser will know that we have new or different information buried in there."

"I would suggest," Worf said, "that you let the Klingon and Vulcan vessels know this information as well."

"I'll ask Captain Kiser to forward it," Riker said. "The Furies are less likely to be monitoring his communications."

"Do you think they're monitoring ours?" Ensign Eckley asked. She was back at her post, looking shaky but calmer.

"We're monitoring theirs, aren't we?" Riker asked.

Picard smiled. "Go to it, Number One. Record the message and encrypt it. Ask for an encrypted message in return. Use my ready room."

Riker nodded and started across the bridge.

"And, Number One," Picard added, "give Captain Kiser my regards as well. Warn him that the house has the advantage so far."

"I will," Riker said. Then he stopped. "But I will also say that I believe we can turn the tables and use the house's advantage to our own. Kiser always did like a long shot."

"Well," Picard said, returning to his command chair. "I hope he likes long shots not just for the challenge."

"Kiser likes a challenge," Riker said, remembering the ironic, contained man he had played cards with a few years before. "But he likes winning even more."

"Good," Picard said, turning back to the screen showing the Furies' ships. "Because that's the only attitude that will get us out of here alive."

Chapter Fourteen

TEN-FORWARD WAS EMPTY. The entire crew was on duty. Families huddled together in their quarters or the specially assigned safe areas that Beverly had set up.

Picard stood at the door. He had forgotten the room was so vast. Behind the bar Guinan worked over something, then turned around and smiled a full smile at him. She had on a purple robe and flowing purple hat that somehow seemed to blend with her dark skin, making her eyes seem intense. Many times Picard had looked into those clear, knowledgeable eyes for help and gotten it. In many ways he considered Guinan one of his best friends, even though he knew very little about her. He just knew that he trusted her completely and over the years she had never let him down. Not once.

"You'd better come sit down," Guinan said, indicating the barstool in front of her. "I don't have table side service anymore." She set a steaming mug of Earl Grey tea on the bar. Hers was real, not replicated. The drink's delicate perfume drifted through the empty room.

"I don't have much time, Guinan," Picard said.

"I know, but you came here for a reason." She slid the tea forward. "Now sit."

He stepped into the room, feeling vaguely guilty. He should be preparing more for the approaching attack, but he had delegated the duties to people with greater expertise in their areas. He had nothing to do but wait.

And worry.

The job of a commander.

"You are preparing for the attack," Guinan said as he approached. "Stop feeling so guilty."

"Is it that obvious?" He climbed onto the barstool. The scent of the tea tickled his nose. He took the mug, felt its warmth against his fingers, and sipped. The bouquet was delicate, as fine as that of any tea he had ever had.

"I doubt it's obvious to anyone else, but I've known you a long time."

"That you have," Picard said. "And you well know I've never faced a situation like this one."

"But you have," she said, the look on her face clearly showing her disagreement. "Every day when you venture into new territory, you face the same decisions you face here."

He shook his head. "No," he said. "This is different. We came into the sector as the advance troop in a

133

war, Guinan. I've dedicated my entire life, my entire career to peace."

"Yet you serve in Starfleet," she said softly.

"Successful Starfleet officers wage peace," he said.

"Sometimes waging peace is preventing universal destruction." She pulled up a chair, pushed her purple hat back, and leaned her elbows on the bar, as if she were the supplicant.

"Sometimes," he said. "I agree. But I can't help the feeling that we are missing something here. The Furies come through the Furies Point and instantly we're at war. Admiral Kirschbaum told me to negotiate, but that felt perfunctory, Guinan. It is as if we have been expecting a battle for eighty years, and a battle is what we're going to get."

"The Furies have terrified this sector for a long time," Guinan said. Her eyes were hooded, her gaze unreadable. He hated it when she was being inscrutable.

"You think we're wrong, don't you?"

"I didn't say that," she said, "but I do think that terror leads to fuzzy decision-making."

"As do I," Picard said. "Yet I have tried to negotiate with them. They will not talk. They are intent on intimidation. They're even sending a beam filled with fake intimidation, forcing our nervous systems into a state of fear."

"Brundage Station was deliberate provocation," Guinan said.

Picard nodded. "But I learned long ago that even given such attempts to start a war, parties can come to peaceful terms."

Guinan lifted her head, her eyebrows together in a

frown. "You're afraid of them," she said as if it were a revelation. "Aren't you?"

"I felt the fear they sent," he said.

She shook her head. "No. I mean, you're really afraid of them. Underneath." She patted her stomach inside her robe. "Down in here afraid."

He licked his lips. It was a question he had been asking himself, and he had been afraid of the answer. Such irony. And it was probably the question that had led him to Guinan in the first place.

"These creatures," he said, "formed the nightmares of my childhood. Paris is full of their images. They grace buildings in the form of gargoyles, fill the Louvre in medieval paintings, are shown being vanquished in the stained glass of ancient churches. We would return home after a visit to that city, and I would dream of gargoyles climbing off buildings, swarming the streets, and coming to get me. When I saw the leader of the Furies, I saw my nightmare come to life."

Guinan took his nearly empty mug and refilled it. But she didn't give it back to him right away. She held it as if considering serving him at all.

He had seen this look before. Guinan had a lot of knowledge about the universe, and while she shared it, she did so judiciously. Always cautious about offending others, always cautious about revealing more than the listener needed to know, she recognized her knowledge as the potential weapon it was.

"Your childhood nightmares confused the evils, Jean-Luc," she said. She wasn't looking at him; she was looking in the mug. "What do you know of gargoyles?"

"Aside from their architectural uses?"

She smiled then, and set the mug before him. The steam rose, coating his hand. "I'm not going to waste our time talking about decorative water spouts."

"I know that they were common on medieval stone structures, and were often imitated as late as the twentieth century."

"That's still architectural," she said. "Gargoyles were placed on buildings to keep the demons out. Jean-Luc, you're confusing your protectors with your enslavers."

He wrapped his hand around the mug, needing the comfort of the warmth. "What do you mean, Guinan?"

"The hatred you feel deep inside is genetic, Jean-Luc." She was looking at him now, her dark eyes filled with compassion. He wasn't certain he wanted to see that. "The Furies terrorized your people thousands of years ago. And not just your people. The Vulcans, the Klingons, even the Ferengi fell prey to them."

Picard nodded. "I know."

Guinan went on. "But do you really, Jean-Luc?" She gave him a look and he wondered if he really did have any understanding.

"After a millennium of rule in this sector, something arrived and overthrew the Furies. The Klingons called them the Havoc."

She stood upright, looking into his eyes. "The Vulcans wrote only of the terror that ensued in the battle. Humans, on the other hand, had several reactions to their protectors. The ancient Greeks made them into gods, Moors and the ancient pagans agreed with the Klingons. Their graphic representations of these 'saviors' was grotesque. Over time they became stylized in garden statuary."

She paused, then said softly, "And gargoyles."

"But if gargoyles were supposed to protect us, then why did I fear them?" Picard asked. "Was that genetic too?"

"Perhaps," Guinan said. "The wrong kind of protection can also be devastating."

He smiled at her. "You say that for a reason."

She smiled back, like a small child caught in a forbidden act. "You know me too well, Jean-Luc. Yes, I say that for a reason."

"This war talk bothers you as well."

She nodded. "Make certain you're going into this properly. Don't fight them just because they terrify you. And don't make up the purpose of their mission here. You don't know yet why they're here."

"I've tried to negotiate," Picard said.

"Really?" Guinan asked.

"Guinan, I've spoken to them twice. I've told them who we are."

"They know that, Jean-Luc. They terrorized your people once. They learned about the Federation the last time they came through here. Telling them who you are is not negotiating."

He took a sip of the tea. "You're right," he said, "we need to speak from a position of strength."

She shook her head. "That's not what I'm saying at all. You need to make a good faith effort with them. You need to find a peaceful compromise, and offer it—with your whole heart."

"My heart hates them, Guinan. You've just said that's bred into me."

"So is battle lust, Jean-Luc. I have never seen that overtake you."

"A rational man overcomes his heritage?" Picard said, with only a bit of irony.

"In a word." Guinan was not smiling. She meant it. She meant it all.

Then Riker's voice broke the silence in Ten-Forward. "Captain Picard to the bridge."

"Acknowledged." Picard looked at Guinan. Then he reached out a hand and clasped hers. "I value your wisdom, old friend," he said, and left.

As Picard entered the bridge, he saw Riker and Data leaning over the science console.

"Sir," Riker said, coming to attention. "The wormhole has changed."

Data hadn't stopped monitoring the screen. Picard's stomach clenched. The light lingering taste of the Earl Grey tea turned sour in his mouth. He wasn't ready for this, not so soon after the discussion with Guinan. He wanted time to think about what she had said.

Time was the only commodity he lacked.

"Analysis, Mr. Data."

"The size of the wormhole has increased by fifty centimeters. It is expanding at a rate of one centimeter every thirty seconds."

Picard couldn't see the change in the wormhole, but he knew that Data's statistics were always accurate.

"I am afraid, sir," Data said, "that the energy output is also increasing, and at a much more rapid rate. Also, the area around the wormhole shows a slight drop in mass."

"Are you getting other readings?" Picard asked. "Do we have any indication that more ships are coming through?"

"No direct indications, sir," Data said. "But these readings match the readings recorded by Brundage Station in the hours before the first ships arrived."

"The five Furies ships," Riker said, "have moved a slight distance away from the mouth of the wormhole to be out of range of the dropping mass."

"That makes sense," Picard said.

"If the pattern follows the one observed earlier," Riker said, "a Furies ship will be able to pass through within six hours."

A ship. Or a fleet of ships?

Picard held himself rigidly, unwilling to let any emotion show. Six hours. Six hours to control his own fears, his own heritage, and the future of his galaxy.

"Have we had word from Mr. La Forge?" Picard asked.

"Yes, sir," Riker said. "He believes that if we alter our shields on the subspace level, we might be able to block the Furies' interspace beam completely."

"Did he give you a timetable?"

"He hoped to have it finished by now, sir."

Picard turned. "Engineering?"

"Go ahead, Captain," La Forge's voice came back strong.

"Are you ready to test your block?"

"Yes, sir. We are implementing it now."

"Good work," Picard said.

As he spoke he could feel the deeper level of fear easing and flowing away, like water down a drain. The relief was almost measurable. He glanced around. He could see that the other members of the bridge were feeling the same way.

He turned to Data. "See that Mr. La Forge's schematics for blocking the Furies' beam are sent to the incoming starships."

"Aye, sir," Data said.

"Sir." Worf's voice was filled with that deep control he had only when a situation was dire. "Two of the Furies ships are breaking away from the others and heading this way."

"Red alert." Picard swiveled on one foot and gazed at the large screen. Three ships remained in position while two others streaked across the darkness toward the *Enterprise*. He didn't want to face the Furies. Not now, not ever. But at least for the moment he was facing them with his fear controlled and his crew alert. At least now they had a fighting chance.

"All hands, battle stations."

He turned and sat down, staring at the screen as the two ships approached. So they were going to try to knock them out before the rest of the help got here. Well, let them try.

"Hail them, Mr. Worf."

"Sir, they are going into attack position."

"*Hail them,* Mr. Worf."

"Aye, sir."

The ships continued forward at their steady pace. The other three ships did not move.

Picard licked his lips. They tasted faintly of Guinan's tea. He had promised her he would try. He was trying now.

"Sir, they are not responding," Worf said.

"Captain, they're emitting their own interspace

fear beams," Riker's voice said calmly. "Almost as if they are trying to increase the intensity of their main beam.

"I do believe," Data said, his gaze on the screen, "that such beams count as an attack in accordance with Starfleet Regulation Four dash—"

"I am aware of the regulations, Mr. Data," Picard said. He gripped the arms of his chair. "Mr. Worf. Have you finished your study of the original Furies ships' ability to take energy from an opponent's weapons?" Picard knew the answer to the question, but he wanted to run through the drill just to clear the final doubts from his mind.

"Yes, sir," Worf said. "Adjustments have been made to all our phasers and photon torpedoes using the records of the original battle. The energy bursts from both weapons will be phased to not allow their absorption."

"So they will not be helped by our firing on them?" Picard asked, not taking his gaze away from the quickly approaching ships on the screen.

Worf grunted, then said, "They will not, sir."

"Then, Mr. Worf," Picard said, staring at the screen, "target phasers. Full spread. Fire when you are ready."

"Yes, sir," Worf said.

And the *Enterprise* rocked from the first impact of the Furies' weapons.

Chapter Fifteen

THE AIR WAS WAY TOO HOT. Deanna had to breathe through her mouth in order to get any air at all. Things coated her tongue and slid down her throat.

Small, slimy things.

Living things.

She tried to spit them out, but couldn't. Part of her craved them, needed them, like she needed the air.

Concentrate, Deanna, her mother said.

Go away, Mother, I'm sleeping.

One should never cling to sleep, dear, when one is having a nightmare.

Deanna peered at the screen in front of her. The *Enterprise* was a small disk in the distance, its main section a thin line beneath the saucer. It seemed insignificant.

Easy to conquer.

She hoped.

Deanna.

Leave me alone, Mother.

I will not, darling. You know I hate to see you upset.

Mother, you never even notice when I'm upset.

I feel your pain as if it were my own, my child. Wake up, now.

A bead of sweat ran down her cheek, and onto her lips. She licked it away, and something small with legs climbed down her throat.

She choked.

Coughed.

Opened her eyes.

Into Beverly Crusher's.

She felt the thread of worry pass through her even as Beverly covered the feeling with a smile.

"Glad to see you awake."

"Mm," Deanna said, not quite willing to say anything yet. The dream still felt close, too close, as if it weren't a dream at all. If she concentrated on it for a moment, she would know what she had missed. Something, something important . . .

"Nightmare?"

Deanna nodded. Beneath Beverly's worry, Deanna felt other emotions swirling, both nearby and far. Fear. Terror. Deep, deep horror. Red hot, burning, able to dissolve her if she let it.

The dream dissipated. "What happened?" she asked, breathless with the emotions swirling inside.

"The Furies sent an interspace beam at the ship—"

" 'Carrying terror on its wings,' " Deanna said.

"What?"

143

Deanna shook her head. "Just something I dreamed."

"No dream," Beverly said. "An attack through interspace. It overwhelmed you. I found you just in time."

Deanna remembered removing her comm badge, making instructions to the computer, heading toward the bridge—and nothing else.

Except her mother's voice.

"My mother's not here, is she?"

"No," Beverly said. "Why?"

Deanna shook her head. An old terror, that of her mother knowing everything. "These fears people are feeling, they're deep, aren't they?"

"Too deep," Beverly said. "I've managed to block the worst of it, and Geordi has developed a screen to block the beam, but we don't know how long that will last." She looked up, checking the medical panel over Deanna's head.

Deanna wanted to ask her what she saw, but her mouth was dry. The emotions swirling underneath were growing. She could feel them below a haze, as if someone had laid a gauze blanket over them.

"Your levels are rising again. I'm going to have to sedate you, Deanna."

"But you woke me, didn't you?"

Beverly nodded. "As things eased. I needed to ask you a question. Then I'll put you back under, deep enough to block the empathic response until you can gain a little more strength. You just need the time."

Deanna could isolate the fears now. Lieutenant Kobe was nearly paralyzed with fear. Ensign Mael was barely containing his deep horror. And someone nearby was losing his mind to terror. She glanced over her shoulder at a man she didn't recognize, unconscious on the next bed.

"He's dying," she said.

"I know," Beverly said. "Sedating him doesn't seem to help. The dreams keep coming to him. Waking him is worse."

Deanna clenched her fists. Even with this blocked level of emotion, she could feel the tide rising, feel it slowly sweep over her. "What's your question?" She had to know before she was unable to think clearly.

"I don't know how to help him, Deanna. He's dying, and there's no physical cause."

"Who is he?" she whispered.

"Lieutenant Young."

"The man who saw the Furies firsthand?"

Beverly nodded.

He was drowning in terror. She could feel it. He had nothing to hold, nothing to keep him from sliding deeper. "Wake him," she said, her voice shaking with the power of his emotion.

"But waking him makes it worse."

Deanna shook her head. "He has to know he's safe. You have to make him feel safe. If you don't, you'll lose him for sure. Do anything you can, but make him feel safe."

Beverly's concern was clearly growing. She obviously knew that Deanna was losing control. "What about you, Deanna? Is that how I help you?"

Deanna shook her head. "My world is different from his. Dreams can be deadly for him; he's subject to the images within his mind. I can't block his emotions—anyone's emotions—in this conscious state. That's why I passed out."

Beverly reached to the small table beside her. She removed a hypospray. "I'll sedate you again, if that's what you want."

Deanna nodded. "Wake me if you need more help. I think I will get stronger quickly."

"I'll do what I can," Beverly said.

She placed the hypo near Deanna's neck, and paused as Riker's voice echoed throughout sickbay: "Battle stations. All hands to battle stations."

After a moment the ship rocked from an impact. Beverly lost her balance, clutched the table, and stayed upright. Deanna clung to the side of the diagnostic table. Waves of fear flooded through her, but she fought to stay conscious.

She had to. Just for a moment.

She remembered what she had learned in her dream.

"Beverly, tell the captain—" The fear levels were growing within her. She could no longer separate out who felt what emotion. She frowned, losing her train of thought.

"Tell him what, Deanna?"

Tell him. Ah, yes. She made herself concentrate on her own words. "Tell him that the Furies are as afraid of us as we are of them. They fear us because they think we're the ones who condemned them to hell."

Beverly looked surprised, but Deanna didn't have time to say any more. The black wave was coming over the top of her. She brought a hand up, reaching for the hypospray.

Beverly understood and gave her the shot as terror flooded through Deanna.

Then the silent, peaceful blackness took her. And this time she welcomed it.

The Fury ships streamed toward the *Enterprise*. Dr. Crusher's potion and Geordi's screens must have worked, because Riker felt the usual adrenaline rush that he always felt before a battle, and nothing else.

No terror.

He knew the *Enterprise* was a match for at least one of those ships, and if they were expecting the crew to be frightened, it would be a match for both ships.

The photon torpedoes soared toward the Fury ships. The ships split, one going above and one going below the *Enterprise,* firing as they went. Riker grabbed the edge of his chair, bracing for impact.

The ship rocked, and the lights flickered for just a moment. Picard stood as if the shot had made him angry.

The photon torpedoes hit one of the ships and missed the other. The bright red flash left a black scar on the ship's front.

"Status, Mr. Data," Picard snapped.

"The shields are holding," he said.

"But they are fluctuating, sir," Ensign Eckley said.

"The ensign is correct," Data said. "Their weapons are apparently designed to disrupt the frequency of our shields. This is something new."

The ships were circling around, as if they were animals stalking their quarry. Riker watched them closely, looking for any detail that would help them win this battle.

"Can you modify the shields, Mr. Data?" Picard asked.

"No, sir," Data said. "I believe this type of work must happen in engineering."

Picard hit his comm badge. "Mr. La Forge—"

"I'm on it, sir," La Forge said.

The ships had turned. "Captain, they're coming around for another attack run," Riker said, his voice firm.

"Mr. Worf—"

"Photon torpedoes locked on target, sir," Worf said.

"Fire!" Picard said.

This time, the torpedoes streaked toward the ships, maintaining their locks. They hit with such impact that both Fury ships rocked and went off course. None of the energy of the strikes was absorbed. In fact, it seemed just the opposite, as if the Fury ships were somehow increasing the impact of the weapons against their sides.

"Bull's-eye," Riker said. He felt almost an extra sense of joy.

"Excellent, Mr. Worf," Picard said. "This time, lock on to the tail section. That appears to be their engines."

"It is, sir," Data said.

"Locked," Worf said.

"Fire!"

The torpedoes shot across space toward the still-recovering ships.

"Sir," Data said, "our shields are at fifty percent. They're failing on decks six and seven."

"Mr. La Forge?"

"I know, sir. Give me ten seconds."

"You have five," Picard said.

"Aye, sir."

The torpedoes hit their marks again, but for a moment nothing happened. Riker held his breath, hoping. Then a bright red glow mushroomed off the first ship's engines.

It was like watching an electrical storm over the surface of the ship. The flashes and red glow kept feeding back and forth, from the front of the ship, then to the back.

Faster and faster, the flashes across the face of the Fury ship increased until finally the ship spun for a moment like a top, completely out of control; then it exploded.

The explosion caught the other ship, and it spun away, firing as it went. The shots flew wild, scattering into space.

Worf grunted. The sound was full of Klingon satisfaction. Riker felt like grunting as well. But he kept his gaze on the other ship. Picard was watching too, an unreadable expression on his face. It was as if he was warring with himself; partly pleased, partly dismayed at the turn of events.

Riker felt only pleasure at the victory.

"Mr. Worf," Picard said, his voice displaying none of the conflict that reigned in his face. "Lock photon torpedoes on the remaining ship."

"Locked, sir."

Riker smiled. Worf had responded so quickly he must have had the lock on before Picard told him to.

"The ship is moving away from us," Data said.

Riker clenched his fists. *Shoot them anyway,* he

wanted to say, but the words went against all his training. They were coming from deep within, from a part of himself he had never met before. From the part the Furies had tapped with their fear weapon.

"Captain," Data said, as if the captain hadn't heard. "The ship is heading back to the other ships near the Furies Point."

Picard said nothing. He watched the screen.

"Shall I fire, sir?"

Again, Picard did not respond. His face, which earlier had been a mix of emotions, held none now.

"Do you think this a ploy, sir?" Riker asked.

Picard let out his breath. He had obviously been holding it.

"We've lost shields on decks four, five, and six," Data said.

That seemed to snap Picard to attention. The ship continued to head toward the Furies Point.

"Shall I fire, sir?" Worf's voice held a barely contained disdain. If he were alone, Worf clearly would have finished off the second Fury ship.

"No, Mr. Worf." Picard returned to his seat. "Unlock torpedoes and resume our previous position."

He did not take his gaze from the screen. Riker glanced at it again. The Fury ship took its place in front of the third ship. Somehow it seemed out of place there, as if the formation were incomplete.

Which, Riker supposed, it was.

"We surprised them, Number One," Picard said. "We won't be able to do that again."

Riker swallowed. The fear returned, if only for a moment. "I know," he said. But the surprise had gotten them this far.

THE SOLDIERS OF FEAR

"Mr. Data," Picard said, "how long until the *Madison* and *Idaho* arrive?"

"Fifty-two minutes, sir," Data said.

The attack had taken less than ten minutes. Riker returned to his chair. Somehow it felt as if it had taken longer than that.

"The Klingon ships will arrive at the same time," Worf said.

"Thank you," Picard said. "Mr. Data, have you an estimate on how long it will take until that wormhole is large enough to let more Fury ships into the sector?"

"According to my calculations, sir, the wormhole will allow a Fury ship to pass through within eighty-one minutes. I do not know, however, what the status of the wormhole is on the other end."

Eighty-one minutes. Riker glanced at the screen. The four ships hung in space, the wormhole invisible near them. It was growing rapidly, and once it reached the right size, an invasion force of unparalleled proportions just might come through to enslave the sector.

And at the moment, the *Enterprise* was the only thing that stood in its way.

He finally understood how the Klingons felt all those centuries ago, facing the invading Herq. Insignificant.

Doomed to failure without a lucky break.

"I hope your estimates are right, Mr. Data."

Data swiveled in his chair. "Why would I report incorrect estimates, sir?"

Riker shook his head. The others on the bridge knew what Picard had meant. If the timing was somehow off, if the wormhole was growing geometrically instead of arithmetically, then the Furies would arrive before the reinforcements. The rout would be ugly.

It would make the attack on Brundage Station look like an evening on Risa.

Chapter Sixteen

"THAT WAS CLOSE," La Forge said. He closed the panel he had been working on, and collapsed in a chair beside it.

Redbay used the laser driver to lock the panel closed. His shirt was plastered to his back. La Forge was right. That had been close. Too close.

When Picard gave them only five seconds to modify the shields, Redbay had thought it impossible. La Forge hadn't even blinked. Two seconds later, five levels of shields had failed, and La Forge was still working. Four seconds after that, La Forge had effected most of the changes.

"I thought you said you needed ten seconds," Redbay had said.

"Captains always shave time off estimates," La

Forge said. "Build a bit of shave into your estimates and you look like a miracle worker."

"I never would have thought of that," Redbay had said.

"Neither would I," La Forge said, moving to a new panel, "but an expert once assured me it would work. And believe me, it has. Every time."

Now La Forge was staring at the main console. Redbay slipped into a nearby chair and called up schematics on his console. Something about the Furies' attack worried him. The shield failures should not have happened, at least not so rapidly. The Furies had somehow interfered with the shield harmonics. Even with the shield failures, though, the block that he and La Forge had set up continued to work. But he doubted it would work much longer.

He glanced over his shoulder at the rest of engineering. Three crew members were rebuilding the damaged portion of the shields. Several others were still working on the warp core. They had lost four members of their staff to the initial terror, not counting the folks who were already out sick.

He turned his attention back to the console before him. "It amazes me that they weren't able to demolish all our shields," he said.

"I'll wager they didn't think they needed to," La Forge said. He looked preoccupied, his fingers dancing across the console as he worked. "They thought we were terrified of them. One blast should have convinced us to surrender."

Redbay nodded. That made sense, but it still didn't get at what was eating him. He was missing something.

154

"But if they come back any time soon, they'll get us," La Forge said. "Our emotion block is eroding. I think it'll deteriorate within ten minutes."

That was what he had been missing. Redbay glanced over at La Forge's console. La Forge was right. They would lose their main protection soon.

"Fixing it shouldn't be hard," Redbay said. On his console he sketched a plan for repair that would leave both the shields and their emotional protection in place.

"Good idea," La Forge said, "but you want to tell me how we're going to do that without shutting down the shields while we repair them?"

Redbay's mouth instantly went dry. The terror had eased for him; he now only felt a slight undercurrent of anxiety, less than he had felt as a cadet in the Academy. But he never wanted to feel that kind of terror again.

Ever.

"It's not possible," Redbay said.

"I know," La Forge said. He took a deep breath, then tapped his comm badge.

"La Forge to bridge."

"Picard here."

"Captain," La Forge said. "We're going to lose our shields in the next ten minutes. I can repair them, but I'll have to shut them off while we're working on them."

"We can't do that, Mr. La Forge."

Redbay could almost believe he heard a slight note of panic in the captain's voice. Picard had understood at once that if they lowered their shields, the wave of terror would again hit the crew full force.

"We can, sir," La Forge said, "if we move away from the Furies Point."

Redbay felt some of the tension in his back ease. La Forge was right. Moving them would help.

"Mr. La Forge," Picard said, "I'm given to understand that the beam the Furies have leveled on us expands at greater distances. We would have to go well into the sector to outfly it. We don't have the time."

"The beam weakens as it stretches, sir," La Forge said.

Redbay was punching numbers into his console as fast as he could. They could survive the pressure if it remained the same as it was here.

"I am not convinced, Mr. La Forge."

Within seconds Redbay found that spot and pointed it out to La Forge on the screen.

La Forge nodded and gave Redbay the thumbs-up. "Sir, we don't have to go far. If we travel seven minutes at warp eight directly away from the Furies Point, we'll arrive at a place where the beam is the same level of intensity as what we're feeling now with the shields up. It won't take us long to fix the shields. I think we'd be back here within half an hour."

There was silence on the other end. La Forge glanced at Redbay.

"Why isn't he answering?" Redbay whispered. He could feel his stomach clamping up at the thought of dropping the terror shield this close to the Fury ships.

"He's checking to see what the reinforcements are doing," La Forge whispered back.

"All right, Mr. La Forge," Picard said. "We will

leave this site for exactly one half hour. No more. Is that understood?"

"Clearly, sir."

"You are making new modifications on the shields, is that correct?"

Yes, sir."

"Then send the changes, encoded, to the incoming starships. We want them to be as protected as they can be when they meet the Furies."

"Aye, sir," La Forge said.

Picard signed off.

"Mr. Anderson," La Forge said, "you will monitor our changes over here, and encode them for the other starships."

Anderson left his post near the warp core. "But sir, the core still needs repair."

"This is top priority, Anderson," La Forge said.

"Aye, sir." Anderson pulled over one more chair, took the remaining console, and waited.

At that moment, the engines wailed, like wind through a cave, as the ship went to warp speed and headed away from the Furies Point.

"I don't like the sound of that," Redbay said. He'd heard warp drives sound a thousand times better on freighters.

"It'll be all right," La Forge said. "She's a good ship."

Redbay frowned at La Forge. "She might be a good ship, but that doesn't mean I trust my life to her when she's damaged."

La Forge grinned. "Neither would I," he said. "But I inspected the warp core. The damage is superficial and very noisy. Our concern is these shields. We have to make these modifications rapidly and precisely in order for the work to be completed in that short timeline."

Anderson glanced at La Forge. He obviously heard the undertone in La Forge's voice. If the repairs weren't made and made correctly, not only would the crew of the *Enterprise* suffer, but so would the crews of the *Idaho* and the *Madison*.

"Nothing like a little pressure," Redbay said, "to keep the job interesting."

La Forge slapped him on the back. "Glad you're enjoying it."

Redbay shook his head. He was doing anything but enjoying it. How had Will managed this all these years? Flying test models of new shuttles suddenly looked very relaxing. His old friend was a very strong person.

The air was thick and teemed with food. Dea had done her job, much to Vedil's surprise, but if she thought that would give her a command position again, she was sadly mistaken. The interior lights were dim, blocked by thick air. The humidity felt good on his scarlet hide.

He sat in his command chair, hooves extended.

Something about the Unclean was bothering him.

He tapped his nails against the arm of the chair, staring at the screen before him. He had called up a screen on the chair arm itself—in this murky atmosphere, seeing beyond the navigator's array was nearly impossible—and was staring at the debris, all that remained of Sse's ship.

Sse had not been the best commander. Most of the

core could not see beyond her fluffy pink fur and wide blue eyes. Not all the Furies were monsters.

Still, he could not blame the destruction of her ship on a commander's error. It had taken thought.

Thought which, his experiments with the young Terran's mind on their guard station had assured him, would have been impossible under the circumstances. The Unclean on that ship should be frozen in fear by now. Not fighting back.

"I want a reading on that ship," Vedil said.

"Vergo, Your Eminence, sir," Prote said, "the shields were disrupted before the *Kalyb* pulled away."

"And the significance of that is?" Vedil asked.

"They should be feeling our power tenfold. I personally have checked our weapon's beam and increased the intensity as by your orders."

Vedil continued tapping his fingernails, the sound dying in the thick mist and damp air. "Should be," he said. "They should be feeling our power. But I see no evidence of this, do you?"

"Vergo, sir," B'el's second head said, "they have released two more communications."

"What do those communications say?" Vedil asked, knowing the answer already.

"We haven't broken their code, Vergo," B'el's second head said. "They are, apparently, changing base language on us with each transmission."

"We have superior intellects," Vedil said. "We should be able to break any and all codes quickly."

"We broke the first, Vergo," B'el's third head said.

"You did not report this."

"Because the communication was insignificant. Simply a report on the status of Brundage Station."

Vedil tapped so hard his nails left tiny dents in the metal. Must he lead them all by their cilia? "If such a communication was insignificant," he said, "why did they encode it?"

"I do not know, Vergo," B'el's first head said.

"Of course you do not know because you do not think! Examine the message again. See if there was a code embedded in the communiqué."

"Yes, Vergo."

"And tell me why those creatures are not terrified of us."

"We do not know how you have come to thisssss conclusssssion," O'pZ said.

"They attacked in a reasonable manner. They are sending encoded communications. They—"

"They are leaving, Vergo," Prote said. His wings unfurled with surprise, catching tiny maggots on the sticky tips.

Vedil returned his gaze to his screen. The ship had turned. Within seconds, it winked out in a flash of colored light.

"See?" Prote said. "We did terrify them."

"It sssseemsss very long to wait after an attack to flee," O'pZ said.

Vedil frowned at the screen, his hide pulling along his forehead. It did seem long. "Examine those communiqués," he said. "The Unclean were prepared for us this time. They waited at the Entrance to Heaven, and they sent this ship which destroyed one of ours. Perhaps this is a ploy."

"Perhaps they are going for more ships," B'el's second head said.

"Perhaps they are fleeing," Prote said.

"Perhaps," Vedil said. Then he leaned back. Unlike most of his crew, he had studied the Unclean. He had studied all the information sent back through the Path to Heaven after the *Rath* had failed in its mission. And since he took their puny guard station, he had continued his study. What he knew was this: Individual Unclean could be broken. The Unclean could be enslaved. But as a group, the Unclean had amazing recuperative powers.

The defeat at the Entrance to Heaven a generation before was another example of Unclean determination.

The Unclean could be fleeing. But Vedil doubted it. They were planning something. And he would have to determine what that something was before the fleet came through the Path to Heaven.

Chapter Seventeen

DESPITE HIMSELF, Picard felt relief as the *Enterprise* moved away from the Furies Point. He had thought the fear was buried thanks to his efforts, Dr. Crusher's, and Mr. La Forge's. Yet the distance was making a huge real—and psychological—difference.

Guinan had been right. This hatred and fear went very very deep.

He sat in his command chair, the restless feeling gone. The bridge crew had focused on the work before them while he had double-checked La Forge's engineering plan and found it sound. Then he had checked on the status of the crew. Most were doing well despite the overwhelming feelings. Most were recovering, and only a few had completely lost control and not yet regained it.

Deanna was one of those. Understandable, of

course, but he needed her. He felt blind without her council. He hadn't realized quite how much he relied on it in situations when his own emotions were untrustworthy.

"We've reached the target point, sir," Ensign Eckley said.

"All stop," Picard said. "Mr. Data, what is the intensity of the Furies' beam at this distance?"

Data hadn't left the science console since the last meeting. The Furies' beam, their wormhole, and their powers were his focus at the moment, in accordance with his orders. And as always, he brought to bear his full and considerable powers.

"It is exactly one-tenth of the strength that it had been in our previous position."

"Excellent," Picard said. Mr. La Forge had been right, as always.

The bridge crew were watching him expectantly at this point. They knew what was going to happen next. Eckley had braced herself, her fingers white on the console.

Picard glanced around. Worf maintained a stoic fierceness. Riker sat beside Picard, hands folded loosely in his lap. They all seemed back to normal. But that would change in a few moments. Even at one-tenth power, that beam was still strong. And was still very capable of undermining the confidence of even the strongest person.

Picard hit his comm badge. "Mr. La Forge, are you ready?"

"As ready as we'll ever be, sir," La Forge said.

"Stand by," Picard said. "Open a channel to the entire ship, Mr. Worf."

Worf gazed down at the console without moving his head. Just a slight flicker of the eyes. Worf was in Klingon battle mode.

"Done, sir."

Picard nodded to him. Then he leaned back in the command chair. He didn't want to sound in any way stressed or alarmed. "This is a general announcement to the *Enterprise* crew and passengers. As most of you are aware, our proximity to the Furies' weapon increases the level of fear on board the ship. Mr. La Forge has made changes in the shields which protected us from most of that fear. Now, however, we will have to drop the shields in order to repair them."

He took a deep silent breath and went on. "We have moved several light-years away from the Furies Point. The level of terror you will feel will be considerably less than the terror you felt earlier. However, the terror will return. Those of you guarding small children will need to explain this as best you can. As for the rest of you, please remember that this increase in the levels of anxiety will be short-lived. I expect you to continue your duties. Picard out."

Riker nodded to him. "Well done, sir."

Picard smiled a smile he didn't feel. "Mr. La Forge," he said. "You have ten minutes."

"We'll be done in eight," La Forge said.

Picard stood. "Ensign," he said to Eckley, "drop our shields."

"Aye, sir," she said.

He took a deep breath.

The fear returned instantly, but he had been right; it wasn't as bad as it had been before. It was a low level of terror, merely an anxiety—although, if he hadn't been prepared, it would have slowly built into a full-fledged panic.

Eckley was pale, but continued at her post.

Riker had stood and gone over to the science station.

Worf stared at the screen ahead of him, as if he could see all the way to the Furies Point.

Picard let out the breath he'd been holding and crossed to the science station too. He still had a lot to do while La Forge worked on the shields.

He stopped behind Data. Somehow it was soothing to see Data checking figures, the screen scrolling before him at a rate too rapid to read.

"Mr. Data," Picard said. "You have been studying this wormhole for some time now. Tell me about it."

Data pushed his chair back from his console. He reminded Picard of a professor Picard had at the Academy, a man who loved to expound on things he knew, a man who was full of more knowledge than Picard could amass in a lifetime.

"The wormhole is clearly artificial, sir," Data said. His long pale fingers still flew across the console. Riker leaned against it, blocking his way, reminding him to place his full attention on the captain and the discussion. "Its movements are too precise to be a natural phenomenon. It is also perfectly oblong, a form in such proportions that does not occur in nature. And it opens at regular, predictable intervals. Also, the energy it gives off contains particles that are refined."

Data glanced back at his screen, then up at Picard. "Despite decades of study, we have been unable to discover why a drop in mass in objects surrounding the Furies' wormhole occurs. But it does so as the hole opens."

"Could it controlled from this side as well as the other?" Picard asked.

"No, sir," Data said, "unless the devices are on the ships themselves. I believe if that were the case, the wormhole would have fluctuated when we destroyed one of their ships."

"I did some tests on this too, sir," Riker said, "when I was looking for the source of the fear beam. The Fury ships are as trapped here as we are. The wormhole is being controlled on the other side."

"How do you know?" Picard asked.

"The wormhole is maintained by a carrier signal that enabled me to scan through it," Data said. "It appears to be controlled by a device on the other side. From what I can tell, the device is located quite near the wormhole entrance. It is quite large, but its projection antenna is small enough that it could be destroyed with a photon torpedo."

Picard spoke quickly. "A photon torpedo could disable this device?"

"I believe so, sir."

"So all we have to do is get close enough to do some precision firing through the wormhole?" Riker asked.

"No, Commander," Data said. "I ran the schematics for that. The particle fluctuations within the wormhole, while they are predictable, would either render the photon torpedo useless in the worst case or, in the best case, throw it off course. The device must be destroyed at an exact point on the other side of the wormhole by a weapon fired from that side."

Picard bent over the science console so that his two

officers could not see his face. He had told Guinan that he wanted a peaceful solution, a solution that would enable them to turn the Furies away without war. She had suggested negotiation. He had tried that, and would again. But if negotiation failed, then he had this.

Destruction of the wormhole.

A suicide mission.

"Do you think we can get the *Enterprise* through there?" Picard asked.

"The odds are six hundred and fifty-six thousand to one, sir," Data said.

"Assuming, of course, that more Fury ships wait on the other side."

"I did not run any other scenario," Data said. "We made that determination."

Picard was cold. He felt better sending in the entire *Enterprise* than doing what he was about to suggest. "And the odds on a single vessel? A shuttlecraft, perhaps?"

"There are too many variables," Data said. "A shuttle, once inside, could make it through the wormhole undetected, but the same particle fluctuations that affect the photon torpedo's trajectory will interfere with the shuttlecraft's. Also its hull structure is weaker than a larger ship's."

"So you're saying that a shuttlecraft has no chance of success," Picard said, almost relieved at the thought.

"No, sir. I am saying that I cannot give you exact odds. But all the scenarios I ran with the shuttlecraft gave odds anywhere between one hundred to one and two to one."

167

"What was the difference?" Riker asked.

"The pilot," Data said. "I believe that a talented pilot, able to compensate for all the variables, would be able to make it through the wormhole and fire the shot."

"I am the most accurate at target destruction done manually," Worf said. He had turned around, his right fist clenched, the only sign of his increased anxiety. "I would like to go on this mission, sir."

"And I am ranked as one of the best pilots in the fleet," Riker said. "And the best on this ship."

Picard looked at his two officers. If he sent them, they would not return. He would have to run the *Enterprise* without them.

"Sir," Data said, "Allow me to add that my abilities in manipulating data, my imperviousness to the Furies' emotion device, and my proven talent at precision flying within one-billionth of an inch would make me the best choice for this mission."

"There is no mission yet," Picard said. "At the moment, this is all speculation. We need to see how Mr. La Forge's device works, whether Dr. Crusher's drugs can keep us calm, and if the Furies are willing yet to negotiate. We still do not know for certain what they want in this sector."

"They say they want total and complete domination of this area of space," Riker said.

Picard nodded. "But you forget the old tool of negotiation. Ask for everything, settle for less."

"I doubt they'll settle for less," Riker mumbled.

"Engineering to bridge." La Forge's voice echoed over the monitor.

"Seven minutes," Eckley whispered in awe.

Picard smiled. Mr. La Forge was quite reliable. "Go ahead, Mr. La Forge."

"We've finished, sir. We're about to bring the shields back on-line."

"Will they block the Furies' terror beam?"

"Absolutely," La Forge said, his voice bouncing with confidence. "On the way over here we also studied the effect that weapon had on our shields. We think we can withstand anything they throw at us, whether it's a terror beam or a modified shield fluctuation shot."

"Or a photon torpedo?" Eckley mumbled. The fear was showing in her increasing disregard for protocol.

Apparently she mumbled loud enough for La Forge to hear. "Anything," he said.

"Excellent, Mr. La Forge." Picard decided to ignore Eckley's comments. He would have to be somewhat lenient after the Furies' beam pummeled them. "Have you sent your schematics to our reinforcements?"

"Yes, sir. In code."

"Good." Picard swallowed. He had been waiting too long to give this next order. "Then turn on the shields. We have work to do."

"Yes, sir," La Forge said.

Picard left the science console and returned to his command chair. He sat down, and as he did he felt stronger, as if he could face anything. Amazing. This must be how he felt most of the time. He only noted it in its absence.

"Mr. Data," Picard said. "When will the other ships arrive at the Furies Point?"

"In twelve minutes, sir," Data said.

Picard smiled. "Ensign Eckley, time our arrival

back there exactly thirty seconds ahead of the other ships."

"Course laid in, sir."

"Engage," he said.

As the ship moved forward, Riker joined Picard in the command area. "This is quite a force that will appear right in front of the Furies."

"That it is, Number One," Picard said. "And unbeknownst to them, we will be protected against their emotion manipulation and their weapons."

"We'll have the advantage."

"And they will know it." Picard stared grimly at the stars streaking across the screen. "This time the Furies will talk to us."

They had to. Picard was not willing to sacrifice his best officers, his ship, or the Federation.

This time, he would make the Furies listen.

Chapter Eighteen

GEORDI'S SHIELD MODIFICATIONS must have worked. Beverly was calm even though the *Enterprise* was approaching the Furies Point.

Beverly glanced at the screen in her research facility. She had it focused not on sickbay but on the stars themselves. She wanted to monitor the proximity of the Furies Point.

Her sedative had worked. She felt good about that and kept repeating it to herself. But it worked best in combination with the shield modifications.

The problem was that the effect of the gas was going to wear off soon. She was trying to modify the gas slightly so that it would last longer. She had downloaded information from Geordi and was working to match the amount of Theragen derivative in the gas to the interspace field they were surrounded by. At best it was a guessing game. But she had to guess right, because she knew the crew needed it during the battle.

They had to have some protection if the shields failed.

Then her assistant Ensign Orne peeked through the doorway. "Dr. Crusher," he said, "you need to see this."

She set the test tube in its tray and stood. Probably Lieutenant Young. She had awakened him, as Deanna suggested, and he had taken one look at Beverly and screamed. Certainly not the reaction any physician wanted.

But it turned out he was terrified of her hair. She called over her assistant Restin, who kept his skull neatly shaved, and Young calmed. Restin had been spending the last hour talking with the boy, and even though his vitals were unchanged, he seemed calmer.

At least he wasn't screaming.

Restin was still talking, slowly and quietly, to Young. Young's readings were the same as they had been when he slept—a good sign, since when he was conscious before his readings had been elevated. He wasn't out of danger, but his odds were improving by the minute.

But Ensign Orne wasn't leading Beverly to Young. She was leading her to Deanna.

Her eyelashes were fluttering, but no REM sleep was recording on the overhead board. She was near consciousness, though, and she shouldn't have been. That sedative Beverly gave her should have lasted much longer.

Beverly took her hand. "Deanna, are you all right?"

Deanna's large eyes opened. They focused instantly, and were clearer than Beverly had expected them to be. "Something changed," Deanna said.

The shields. So part of Deanna's sleep had been instinctive protection against too much emotion.

"I lightly sedated the crew a while back, and Geordi has modified the shields again to more completely block the Furies' beam."

"People are still frightened," Deanna said, "but not like they were."

"They shouldn't be frightened anymore," Beverly said.

Deanna shook her head just a little. The movement was almost imperceptible. "It's normal," she said. "'Frightened' is too big a word. People are worried. As they always are when the *Enterprise* is in danger."

And Deanna was obviously used to that level of worry. Beverly felt herself relax.

"Except." Deanna looked over her shoulder. "That boy. He's still terrified."

"We're doing all we can," Beverly said.

"It may not be enough." Deanna closed her eyes and sighed. "Is the *Enterprise* in danger?"

"We're heading back to the Furies Point—to take them on, I suspect. But knowing Jean-Luc, he will try to talk with them again."

"Again?" Deanna opened her eyes and pushed herself up on her elbows. "He shouldn't negotiate without me."

"You were hardly in any condition to help him, Deanna."

"But I can help him now," she said.

Beverly shook her head. "I can't let you. Only an

hour ago, you weren't in much better shape than that boy."

Deanna looked at him, her face filled with compassion. "If I stay here, I will have to help him. And I'm not sure I can delve into that level of emotion just yet. Besides, the Furies are complex beings. I've been dreaming of them."

"Dreaming?" Beverly asked. She was always a-mazed at the twists and turns Deanna's abilities took when she encountered a new race.

She nodded. "They're in my subconscious like a pattern. It must be the human part. But that opens the Betazoid part. I have dreamed about being on their ship."

"You said they were afraid of us."

"They are," Deanna said. "But it is a different kind of fear than the terror they've been projecting toward us. It is the nagging fear that somehow, over the millennia, we have grown even stronger than we were when, they think, we drove them out of heaven."

Beverly laughed, although she didn't mean to. "You're kidding?"

"Not at all," Deanna said. "And it got worse for them in the last eighty years. The generation since their defeat at the hands of the original *Enterprise* has felt weak. This trip is to prove their strength as well as enable their return to this section of space."

"Rather like a Klingon loss of honor."

"Rather," Deanna said. Her voice held just a trace of irony. "On a grander scale. From what I can tell, their entire culture is based solely on returning here."

She swung her legs off the bed. "I have to go to the bridge."

"I wouldn't recommend it," Beverly said. "If the shields break down, if the gas clears, you will be overwhelmed again. Your system still hasn't completely recovered. It may not be able to take another shock like that, and I might not be able to help you."

Deanna was watching Lieutenant Young. His mouth was open and a thin line of drool ran from his lips to the pillow. He was as close to mindless as a human could be and still feel. Even Beverly knew that, and she was no empath.

"I understand," Deanna said. "But it's better to risk my life and be at the captain's side than risk losing this opportunity with the Furies."

"Deanna," Beverly said, "Jean-Luc is used to diplomatic dealings. He can do this without you."

"I'm not so certain," Deanna said. "He is having the same trouble being calm as the rest of the crew. But you know the captain. He won't show it."

Beverly suppressed a smile. It was so like all of them to believe they were indispensable. That was one of the things she liked about working with this crew. Usually.

"But you are being overwhelmed at the detriment of your own health," Beverly said softly.

"Not right now," Deanna said. "Besides, I am used to thinking through intense emotion brought in from the outside. He is not. If something were to change, he might need my counseling more than ever."

She had a point, much as Beverly hated to admit it. The only person on the ship used to working through a haze of outside imposed emotion was Deanna. And to try to face the Furies without her was foolish. What had Jean-Luc said when he learned that Deanna was in sickbay? Hadn't he mumbled something about needing her?

"All right," Beverly said. "It's against my medical judgment to let you go, but these are extenuating circumstances."

"Thanks," Deanna said. She swung her legs off the bed. "I'll be all right. I promise."

Beverly nodded. She even smiled. But she watched carefully as Deanna left the room, memorizing each step, each movement.

Beverly had a hunch she might never see Deanna alive again.

The bridge crew was calmer. They were going about their business with a rapidity that meant their movements were unencumbered by unfamiliar emotions.

Picard felt the shift inside himself. Instead of dreading the meeting with the Furies, he welcomed it. If he could convince them to negotiate, then all would be solved.

He didn't want to think about Data's other solution.

At least, not yet.

The *Enterprise* dropped out of warp, and took up its previous position, facing the four remaining Fury ships. They looked smaller somehow. The loss of the fifth ship had diminished them. Or maybe it was the loss of the fear. Something a person fears always looks bigger.

"Mr. Data," Picard said. "What is the change in the wormhole's growth?"

"In fifteen minutes," Data said, "it will be large enough for Fury ships to pass through."

That made Picard pause. The growth in the wormhole had gone slightly quicker than Data's earlier estimates. Picard didn't know if the other ships had been in contact with the Furies on the other side of the wormhole; if so, then perhaps they had escalated their arrival once the fifth ship was destroyed.

Or perhaps Data's calculations had been in error. He had warned that some of them were based on speculation.

Like the calculations he made about destroying the wormhole. Nothing was certain.

"Fifteen minutes is all we need," Picard said, sounding more confident than he felt. He hadn't been able to talk with the Furies before, but then, as Guinan pointed out, his whole heart hadn't been in it. This time, with the reinforcements behind him, he might be able to talk with them. He hoped that talking was all he needed.

The turbolift door hissed open. Picard turned. He hadn't ordered anyone onto the bridge.

"Deanna," Worf said, his voice filled with a kind of awe.

She was paler than usual, her eyes taking up most of her face. Picard would have thought that she was recovering from a long illness if he hadn't known that she had been fine just the day before.

She smiled at Worf, the expression filling her face with radiance. That smile put not just Worf but Picard at ease. He hadn't really realized how much he counted on her in situations like this one.

"Worf," she said. She went down the two steps toward her seat, and touched Riker's hand as she did so. He looked relieved that she had returned. No, "relieved" was too small a word. He looked as if a well-loved member of his family had just returned from a long voyage.

"Welcome, Counselor," Picard said. "I trust Dr. Crusher gave you a full bill of health."

Troi's smile had a touch of the imp to it. "She let me out of sickbay," Troi said, "does that count?"

"Enough for now," Picard said.

Riker glanced at the screen and then at her. "Deanna, do you think it wise—?"

"Will," she said, and he stopped.

"The *Madison* and *Idaho* have arrived," Worf said. "They have taken positions behind us on either side."

More tension left Picard's shoulders. Part of him, the worried part that the Furies' beam had dislodged, had wondered if the other two starships would arrive on time.

Their arrival took the attention off Counselor Troi.

"I thought the Klingons would be with them," Riker said.

"They are," Worf said, his voice controlled but his annoyance somehow clear anyway. "They have just decloaked. One ship is above us. The other below. It is the Vulcan ship that is delayed."

"Two Klingon ships," Picard said. "Good."

"The Klingons clearly believe this too important to trust to one vessel," Worf said, subtly reminding them all about the honor still at stake.

"So much the better." Picard uncrossed his leg and put his hands on the arm of his chair. He was about to stand when Troi's fingers brushed his sleeve.

"When you speak to them," she said softly, "remember that they are frightened."

At first he thought she was talking about the other ships that had just arrived. Then he realized she meant the Furies.

"This is very important to them," she said, by way of explanation.

"It is to all of us," Picard said.

She shook her head. "No, they believe our remote ancestors were the ones who kicked them out of this area of space."

Picard stared at her for a moment, letting what she said sink in. If he needed it, he would use it. But now that the *Idaho* had arrived, he had another weapon, too. He had the poppets from the Fury ship *Rath*.

He patted Troi's hand as a way of thanks and stood. He adjusted his shirt, and stepped before the screens. "Hail the Fury vessels, Mr. Worf, and when you do make certain all our ships hear this message as well."

"Aye, sir."

Picard hesitated a moment. He needed to add one more element into this equation. "And Mr. Worf, send this all subspace Priority One to Starfleet. I want the entire sector listening in."

"Done, sir," Worf said. "The main Fury ship is answering your hail."

"On screen." As Picard said the words, Riker stood and stopped a half-step behind him. Troi did the same on the other side. He was flanked by two officers. That, combined with the reinforcements, would make this a united front.

The Furies would know that the Federation was no small primitive planet, to be awed and enslaved by beings who thought themselves more powerful.

The screen blinked on, and the creature he had

spoken to before reappeared. Its hide was a duller red, and the edges of its features seemed hazy.

"That's the best I can do," Worf said. "The haze appears to be something aboard their ship."

"Bugs," Troi whispered, and as if to confirm her words, a swarm of tiny black gnatlike insects flew out of the curve of the creature's horns.

"I suppose you would like to talk," the creature said, its voice heavy with irony. "I heard this is how you fight your enemies. You talk them into submission."

"We negotiate," Picard said.

"Negotiate." The creature hooked a maggot on its nail and then slid it off with its teeth. Picard suppressed a shudder. Even without their beam, these creatures plugged directly into his subconscious. Although at the moment, he was registering more disgust than fear. This must be the level of fear that the original *Enterprise* crew felt, before the Furies had their fear beam.

"What is there to negotiate?"

At last. A small breakthrough. "You came through that wormhole because you wanted something," Picard said. "Instead of fighting for that something, perhaps we can supply it. Our beliefs ask us to find a peaceful solution first."

"You destroyed our ship," the creature said.

Riker clenched a fist. Picard straightened his shoulders. As if they deserved blame for this situation. The Fury knew that they had provoked the attack.

"You murdered the crew of our research station," Picard said slowly, making sure he had the force he wanted behind his voice.

"Not all of them," the creature said with a leer. Another creature moved across the screen behind it. The creature had three heads, each different. One looked like a Klingon Scarbaraus statue.

"The KdIchpon," Worf said softly, as if in awe.

Picard refused to be goaded. Or terrified. "We destroyed one of your ships, and you attacked our station. We are even. That seems a good place to begin negotiations from."

Troi brushed his sleeve again. Picard glanced at her. She was staring at the screen, her eyes black coals, her skin even paler. He had forgotten about her human side. She had to see the demons that he saw as well as feel the emotions around her.

"What have we to negotiate?" the devil creature asked.

They were at least talking. Picard had to give them that. Talk was always the beginning of diplomacy.

"They're stalling," Troi whispered so softly that he almost didn't hear her.

His mouth went dry. "You came through the worm-hole in search of something. Perhaps we can help you with that search, without bloodshed."

"Oh, you will help us with that search," the creature said.

"Captain," Troi whispered. "He is playing with you."

The creature apparently heard her. It grinned, the look revealing nasty, slime-covered teeth. "She is correct, Picard. We toy with you. We came through the Entrance to Heaven in search of former glory. It is not something you can give us. It is something that can only be won."

Picard latched on to the word "won." "And if we lay down our arms, face you peaceably?"

"Captain!" Worf said, clearly appalled.

"Then we gain even more glory," the creature said, "for you consider us too mighty to fight. Will you surrender, Captain Picard?"

Picard lifted his chin. "Never," he said. "You will never achieve glory, former or future. We defeated you once in battle, and we shall do so again."

He took a deep breath. "I have something to offer you in negotiation. We have an escape pod full of the poppets from the *Rath*. I will turn them over to you to assure you of our goodwill."

"What!" the leader of the Furies shouted, jumping toward the camera. "We will take them from you. You will die!"

Picard stepped back. He had not expected such a reaction. He knew this conversation was at an end. He now had the upper hand, and it would stay that way for the moment.

He whirled and motioned Worf to end the communication. Picard was no longer frightened. He was angry. The Furies believed that only the enslavement of the races on this side of the galaxy would enable them to obtain glory? They would quickly learn how impossible glory was going to be.

"Mr. Data, how many minutes until that wormhole opens?"

"Ten, sir. But—" Data paused, leaned over the console. "The energy emissions are increasing." He slid his chair back, looking as stunned as an android could look. "My calculations were inaccurate, sir."

"They're coming through now?" Riker asked.

Data shook his head. "No, sir. But I estimated a single ship would come through the wormhole. According to these new readings, they are sending ships in waves. Hundreds of ships. It is only the first that will arrive in ten minutes."

"They're storming us as if we were a beachhead," Picard muttered.

"What?" Riker asked.

Picard shook his head. "It is an old saying, Will. One that once worked in Earth's favor."

But this time it wouldn't work in Earth's favor. The *Enterprise*, the *Madison*, and the *Idaho*, along with the Klingon ships, could probably destroy the four ships guarding the wormhole. But after that, hundreds—

—maybe thousands—

—of ships would come through.

The five battle-scarred ships, along with more reinforcements, would be no match.

No match at all.

"Captain," Riker said softly. "We need to close that wormhole."

Picard nodded. He knew that. But until this moment he hadn't been willing to face the fact that he was going to have to send one of his people to their death. But now he had to.

The question was, which one?

Chapter Nineteen

WORF STUDIED THE SECURITY CONSOLE before him. The two Klingon ships, *DoHQay* and *HohIj,* were revolving on the schematic before him. The *DoHQay* was captained by Krann, son of Huy', of the House of Thorne. Krann was a good commander, not very daring, but protective of Klingon honor. The *HohIj* was captained by KoPoch, son of Karch, of the House of Kipsk. KoPoch was a strong commander with a gift for risk. They were both good additions to this force.

But the two houses were at war with each other. It was a brilliant ploy on the part of Gowron. Send the leaders of the warring houses here. Have them outdo each other in battle, and probably die. Both houses would retain their honor, and the feud would end. Three problems solved and, if it succeeded and the

Furies were turned back, Gowron would again be a hero.

The man sometimes was a visionary.

Worf frowned.

But if it failed, the two ships would turn on each other instead of the Furies, and Klingon honor would be even further destroyed.

He looked up as Captain Picard ended his communication with the Fury. Worf ended the transmission and wiped the schematics of the ships off his board.

They could not let this go to war.

The Federation was not able to fight as vicious a fight as was needed. Gowron was more concerned with his own problems than with saving the sector from the Furies. He probably believed that his secondary force would do the real fighting.

Commander Riker, with too much fear in his voice, reminded the captain that someone had to destroy the wormhole. Worf did not fear the task. He welcomed it.

The captain looked directly at Worf. Worf straightened, determined to look like a warrior.

"Sir," Data said. "A Fury ship has come through the wormhole."

The captain whirled, Worf apparently forgotten. "On screen."

The ship flying through the wormhole was larger than the ships already guarding it.

"I thought you said fleets would be coming through," Riker said to Data.

"They are," Data said. "They are apparently entering one ship at a time in sixty-five second intervals."

"How many ships are you reading, Data?"

"I count a minimum of one hundred ships, sir," Data said, "and that only covers the ships which my sensors can pick up. At a distance through the wormhole, the readings become hazy."

"Were your readings on the device on the other side hazy?" Riker asked.

"No, sir," Data said. "Those are accurate. I used—"

"We have no time, Mr. Data," Picard said.

Worf agreed. Very soon another ship would come through the wormhole. They would lose their advantage if the captain did not act.

"Sound the red alert, Mr. Worf."

"Aye, sir," Worf said. He tapped in the command, and within seconds the lights all over the ship glowed red. "Captain. We have only a few moments. Send me through the wormhole."

Data stood. "No, sir. I am the logical choice."

"Your analysis said a skilled pilot was needed," Worf said, letting some of his anger lash at Data. "My instincts are superior to your programming. A skilled pilot knows when to use speculation—"

"Mr. Worf," the captain cautioned.

Worf stopped.

"Mr. Worf has a point," Data said, "but I do not feel the emotional effects of the Furies' beam. I would remain rational throughout."

"Thank you, Mr. Data," Picard said, "but I need you here. If we lose our screens, I need someone here who can still think clearly and take control."

"You need all of us here," Riker said. "But you'll have to choose someone, and quickly."

Worf looked at him. Riker was one of the best pilots

in Starfleet. His record was better than Worf's. Everyone knew that. But he didn't have honor to defend. He had less at stake. And a warrior with a blood vengeance was always more powerful than one without.

"Captain, I have honor to avenge," Worf said. "The Klingons were defeated by the first Fury ship. Let me return honor to my people!"

"Another ship is about to come through, sir," Ensign Eckley said.

"Mr. Worf," the captain said, "I want you to take the shuttlecraft *Polo* with a full contingent of armaments. Have Mr. La Forge download the shield modifications into the shuttle's computers."

"Aye, sir." Worf pivoted, and headed for the turbolift.

"You are not dismissed, Mr. Worf."

Worf halted. He had felt at odds with the captain ever since this mission began. His sense of what was needed obviously differed from Picard's. "I am sorry, sir."

"You shall use the shuttle *Polo* as a shield for Commander Riker." Picard's voice softened as he turned to face Riker. "You are the best pilot on the ship, Will."

"Thank you, sir," Riker said.

"I am the better shot," Worf said, unable to remain silent.

The captain nodded. "I know. Which is why you will defend Will's shuttlecraft," Picard said.

"Sir," Riker said, "Lieutenant Sam Redbay from engineering—he's a damn good pilot. He'll be able to fly third cover."

"Good," Picard said, nodding. "Have him provide defense from the shuttle *Lewis*."

"Captain," Worf said, knowing he had only one more chance at convincing Picard, "Klingons are used to dying for honor. Humans are not."

Picard was standing almost at attention. Deanna looked lost beside him. Her face was blank, her eyes distant as if she couldn't bear to watch what was happening in front of her.

Suddenly Worf's words came back to him. A Klingon commander would not think twice about sending one of his men to die in battle. The captain obviously felt burdened by it.

"I know, Mr. Worf," Picard said. "I shall depend on that finely honed sense of honor to get Commander Riker through the wormhole, alive, and his shuttle intact."

Worf raised his head as the realization hit him. Captain Picard did not believe any of the shuttlecraft would return. He was sending out his troops to die with honor. It did not matter who fired the final shot, only that the final shot was made.

"I shall do everything within my power to make certain Commander Riker enters the wormhole," Worf said.

"I'll destroy that device," Riker said. "You can count on it, sir."

"I am counting on it," Picard said, softly. "Dismissed."

Riker joined Worf.

Both of them looked squarely at their captain, and he returned their stare. It lasted only a moment, but it was long enough for Worf to understand that Picard was very proud of both of them.

It was an honor Worf would take to his death. As a warrior he could be no more blessed.

Deanna took a step toward both of them and then stopped. A tear was streaking down her cheek. Beside him, Riker smiled to her.

All Worf could bring himself to do was nod. This was his proudest moment. Deanna was strong. She would survive.

Together they turned and headed for the turbolift.

The door slid open and they entered, turned, and faced the bridge as a unit. All eyes were on them.

Deanna stood beside Picard, her arms hanging at her side. Worf had never seen her look so upset.

"Good luck," Picard said.

"Thank you, sir," Worf said.

Riker glanced up at him and smiled. "It is," he said, giving voice to the traditional Klingon battle cry—and meaning it, "a good day to die."

Chapter Twenty

DOZENS OF PERSONNEL flooded the shuttlebay. Technicians crowded around all three shuttles. Other people were taking notes.

Redbay noted as he glanced around that one woman was putting emergency medical kits on each shuttle. One-man medical kits, the kind that a person could use with one hand on the console. Not very effective. The kits were often used on missions in which the pilot's health was not an issue.

Staying alive was.

Redbay's mouth was dry. Picard had ordered him to report to Commander Riker in shuttlebay, nothing more. Redbay assumed he would get more orders when he arrived.

The conversation, though, usually so high in a

situation like this, was muted. People seemed to be speaking only when necessary.

Another sign of a serious mission.

Of course, how could the mission be anything else? The Furies were out there, waiting, literally growing stronger by the minute. Any mission at this point would be serious.

Will Riker and Lieutenant Worf were standing near the computer tactical display terminal on the interior wall. An ensign beside them sighted Redbay and tapped Riker on the shoulder, pointing his way.

Riker turned. He had a look in his eyes that Redbay had seen before, a steely determination that made Riker seem twice as powerful as usual. No longer the roommate from the Academy, no longer the jet-dogfight partner, no longer the good friend. This was Riker the warrior, ready to do battle.

And when Riker was like this, he was usually very serious and very, very determined.

So Redbay forced himself to grin. If nothing else he could keep the tension of this down to a reasonable level.

Riker motioned for him to join them. Redbay made his way around the technicians, ignoring the argument near the diagnostic computer, an argument he could have settled with few words, and hurried toward Riker. When he reached Riker's side, Riker clapped a hand on his shoulder.

Will had only done that once before.

A dogfight run the cadets had to fly because the Federation base near Chala IV was under attack.

They had thought they were going to die that day.

So Will thinks we are going to die. No wonder he had the look.

"I only have a few minutes to brief you," Riker said. "The longer we wait, the more Fury ships come through that wormhole."

"There are six ships now," Worf said.

Redbay tensed. He glanced at the monitor. Sure enough, six ships hovered near the wormhole opening. "They're coming through, quicker than expected?"

Riker nodded. "About one a minute. We don't know how long they'll wait before they attack."

"That's where we come in, I take it," Redbay said.

"Lieutenant Data has found a way to destroy the wormhole," Worf said. "However, it cannot be done with the *Enterprise.* It must be done by a sure shot from a shuttlecraft."

Redbay swallowed. He'd seen Worf's records. He knew Will's. All three of them were crack shots and top pilots.

"Here's the schematic." Riker tapped the console. A computer simulation of the wormhole appeared. It looked like the horn of plenty Redbay's mother had put on their dining-room table every fall, even in Nyo when fall didn't really exist.

The six ships hovered around the small side of the horn. A small red dot on the other side of the horn flashed.

The target.

"That's the power source," Riker said, pointing at it. "Hit it just right and there will be a feedback loop that will destroy the wormhole, and the Furies will no longer have a path to us. The problem is the shot. I figure we only have one chance at it."

He tapped the console again, and a blue dot appeared. It was near the mouth of the horn.

On the other side.

The shooter would have to go through the wormhole, past all the Furies' ships, into enemy territory. Suddenly he understood the reason for Will's determination.

This made every other mission Redbay had flown look like a cakewalk.

"All right," Riker said. "Data believes that the shuttles can make it through the wormhole without being detected. The Fury ships in there are in a form of stasis field, crowded one right after another. The shuttle won't be. It should make it through in one-hundredth of the time they are taking coming the other way."

Redbay nodded. "Do we have enough firepower?"

"One photon torpedo is all it will take," Riker said. "Each shuttle is equipped with more than that."

"Only one shuttle will go through the wormhole," Worf said. "The other two will provide cover." He brought his head up and met Redbay's gaze. Klingons were naturally fierce; Worf even more so. "You had better be as good a pilot as Commander Riker says you are."

Redbay glanced at Riker, who didn't even grin. "He is, Worf. Trust me."

"So I am taking one of the shuttlecrafts," Redbay said, "and doing what?"

"Providing cover for me," Riker said.

"You're going through?"

Riker nodded. "You and Worf will make sure I get inside. If the wormhole doesn't collapse in four minutes after that, then you'll have to try. But I doubt that will be necessary. The tricky part is getting into the wormhole and through it. The shot is easy."

"After you destroy the power source," Redbay asked, "how long will it take the wormhole to collapse?"

Riker bent over the console and tapped it once more, and the screen went dark. He didn't say any more.

He didn't need to.

A suicide mission.

Picard was sending his second-in-command because he didn't trust anyone else to get the job done.

With ships coming through the wormhole one every minute, the odds of Redbay and Worf surviving were small too.

But not as small as Riker's.

"You are taking the shuttlecraft *Lewis*," Worf said. "I will be in the *Polo*. I shall head for the wormhole at top speed. When the Furies try to intercept me, I shall veer off."

"Then you will do the same, Sam," Riker said. "When they move to intercept, veer off. You'll take at least one of their ships with you. I will be right behind you. Only I'll go in."

It sounded so easy.

It sounded like it might work.

"What about the starships?" Redbay asked.

"They all will be doing variations of the same maneuvers, trying to pull Fury ships away from the wormhole," Riker said. "The Furies won't fall for this very long, which is why we have to move quickly. You'll be on Worf's tail. Questions?"

Redbay shook his head. What was there to question? He and his best friend were going to die in the next few minutes. It was that simple.

"Good," Riker said. "The shuttles are equipped with the diagram of the target. They also have modified shields. I have no idea how well those shields will hold up with the Furies in close range. In case it gets too much, Dr. Crusher has provided us with her calming gas. I suggest that we not use it unless absolutely necessary. She claims it has no effect on motor skills, but I'm not so certain."

"Sometimes fear has an effect on motor skills," Redbay said, remembering La Forge as he fell out of the Jeffries tube.

"Which is why we're equipped with the gas." Riker turned and faced them both. "You both ready?"

"Yes, sir," both Worf and Redbay said at the same time.

Riker nodded. "Let's do it."

Without another word he turned and walked quickly toward the center shuttle. Worf strode toward the left shuttle.

Redbay stood for a moment watching his best friend move toward his certain death. He knew without a doubt he would never see Riker again. But he couldn't leave it like that.

"Will!"

Riker glanced around, but kept walking.

"I want a rematch when you get back. I saved that last dogfight."

Riker grinned. "You got it."

Redbay ran toward the remaining shuttle. He was the best pilot in Starfleet, and one of the best shots. He was going to prove just how good he was by giving Riker the best cover possible.

And helping him close that wormhole forever.

Picard moved his shoulders trying to ease some of the tension. The bridge seemed empty without Will and Worf. Data still manned the science console, and Counselor Troi remained on the bridge. But Data's news about the wormhole was not good—more ships lined up inside, waiting to come through—and Troi was looking more and more strained with each passing moment.

The five-way conversation with the other two starship captains and the captains of the Klingon ships hadn't helped. They all agreed that Mr. La Forge's schematics helped them, and they also agreed on the coded attack plan Picard had sent them, but the agreement had ended there. Both captains Higginbotham and Kiser commended Picard on his negotiation skills. The Klingon captains believed that negotiating had been a waste of time. They seemed amazed that they could agree upon anything.

Privately Picard agreed with the Klingons. If he hadn't tried to negotiate, Will might have had a better chance of getting through that wormhole.

But if Picard hadn't tried to negotiate, then he never would have been able to live with himself. He would have forever wondered if going to war first had been the best choice.

Now he had no doubts.

Seven Fury ships hung in space around the wormhole. Another one was due at any second. He knew that Will knew the importance of speed. He hoped that speed would be possible.

"Sir," Data said. "The lead Fury ship is hailing us."

Picard's stomach clamped up like a vise. Now what were they trying? "On screen. And make sure the other ships are getting this transmission."

"Done, sir."

The face of the leader of the Fury ships filled the screen. The image seemed clearer this time, as if the haze and fog on the other side had lifted. And the horned captain of the Furies didn't seem as self-assured.

"You claimed to have the souls of those from the *Rath?*"

So that what this was all about. Maybe there was a slight hope yet of stopping this without losing good people to the fight. Maybe those poppets Kirk had saved would save the day here.

"We do. They have been kept safe and brought here. We had hoped to have a peaceful exchange."

The horned captain on the other side glanced at someone offscreen, then back at Picard. "Which ship are they on?"

Picard shook his head, then laughed. "No information. You stop your fleet from coming into our sector and we'll talk. Not before."

"Picard." The Furies' captain stood, its face almost red with anger. For the first time Picard saw the poppet doll hanging at its side. It was a replica of the

197

being wearing it. "If those souls are destroyed or harmed, I personally will kill you slowly and very painfully."

"If those souls are destroyed," Picard said, his voice very level and firm, "you will be the one destroying them. Not I."

Picard signaled for the communication to be cut off. All hope of stopping this fight was now gone.

But if it was a fight they wanted, then a fight they would get. He turned and moved back to his command chair and sat down.

"Shuttles are ready and launching," Ensign Eckley said.

"Mr. Data, signal the other ships to move into position," Picard said. "It's imperative that we move those Furies away from the wormhole. Now."

"Aye, sir," Data said.

Troi's hands clutched the arms of her chair.

"Sir," Eckley said, "another ship is coming through the wormhole."

On screen, the eighth Fury ship took a position near the opening to the wormhole. Eight ships against five. The original *Enterprise* had had trouble defeating just one Fury ship. There was no time left.

"Battle stations," Picard said. "Ahead full impulse. Target photon torpedoes and fire on my mark."

On screen the other two starships moved into position. As planned, the Klingon ships turned and flew away from the battle site. Once they had gone a respectable distance, they would cloak. With luck, the Furies would think that the Klingons had retreated, not realizing that the Klingons had cloaking ability. The Klingons would then attack the Fury ships from behind and above, decloaking at the last minute as they fired.

But the main target of the Furies' attack would be the *Enterprise,* and the moment the ship moved forward, the Furies turned toward it, as planned.

Rays of light extended from the Fury ships, green this time, as if the different color marked different weapons.

The *Enterprise* rocked as the first impact of Fury fire hit the shields.

"Damage, Mr. Data."

"None, sir. The shields are holding," Data said.

Picard took a deep breath. The fight had truly begun. He just hoped it would end here and not on Earth.

"Fire," he said.

Chapter Twenty-one

RIKER'S HANDS MOVED on the shuttlecraft controls as if he were piloting any normal shuttle mission. But he wasn't. This was the most important mission of his career.

Of his life.

If he succeeded, he—William T. Riker—would have stopped the Furies from invading his sector. He would have kept thousands, maybe millions from dying. After his own personal glimpse of hell, he thought it almost worth the cost.

He grinned at himself. He had to qualify the thought, because he wasn't Klingon. He believed in dying with honor, but he would rather not die at all. And if he could help it he wouldn't. He didn't know how he'd get back from the other side of that wormhole, but he'd find a way.

The shuttlebay doors opened. He settled into the familiar shuttle pilot's chair, his hands still dancing across the controls. Oddly enough, he wasn't frightened. Geordi had modified the shields, and that had helped, but that wasn't all of it.

This last mission was the right mission. Not even dying scared him. Not even the possibility of dying scared him.

Not anymore.

Some things were worse than death. And living in a galaxy run by the Furies was one of them.

As he cleared the shuttlebay doors, he pulled up a schematic of the entire area around the Furies Point. Eight Fury ships now encircled the wormhole. Worf was moving as planned at an angle slightly away from the Furies. Redbay flew his shuttle on the same line. Riker dropped into line. Their trajectories should convince the Furies that they were trying to escape. Yet all three shuttles would remain close. They would be prepared to fly into that wormhole at a moment's notice.

Now it all depended on how well Picard's plan worked.

It had to work.

For all their sakes.

Riker kept on the line, monitoring the others. Adrenaline started pouring through him. He was ready for a fight. These few seconds before battle were always the hardest.

The *Enterprise* moved directly at the Furies Point. The *Madison* followed. When they got in close the *Enterprise* would turn to port and the *Madison* would go to starboard on attack runs.

The *Idaho* circled high, a lone graceful starship, apparently on her own path. Gradually, the *Idaho* also closed in on the Furies Point.

The Furies had a lot to watch.

The two Klingon ships had also taken a direction that would allow the Furies to think they had been running away. They were now cloaked, and Riker knew that within moments they would reappear firing.

Then the closest Fury ship shot at the *Enterprise*. The burst of light was sudden and startling. Riker felt a welcome tension in his arms and shoulders.

The battle had started.

He kept on his line, a small ship, unnoticed. He tried to be as invisible as possible, as if willing it would help.

The *Enterprise* returned fire on the closest Fury ship. The *Idaho* swooped down and fired also.

The battle had been joined.

Four of the Fury ships took positions against the *Enterprise* and *Idaho*. The *Madison* took on two others, and space was filled with explosions and flashes of light. Phaser fire connected the ships like deadly lifelines.

"Klingons?" Riker whispered. "Where are you?"

A Fury ship in front of the *Enterprise* exploded in a burst of colored light. Debris flew in all directions.

One down, but thousands more in that wormhole to deal with.

Riker glanced at the shuttles in front of him. Worf and Redbay seemed all right.

For the moment.

The *Enterprise* turned its weapons on the nearest

ship, with the *Madison* lending her firepower. From this distance, the starships appeared to have complete control, but Riker knew the *Enterprise* was taking a pounding.

He hoped the shields would hold.

And that Beverly's drug would work if they didn't.

"Come on, Klingons," he whispered. He hoped the shields worked for them too. If they didn't, there might be a disastrous repeat of the first fight at the Furies Point.

He wished he could see Worf. He wondered if Worf was as worried about the Birds-of-Prey as he was.

He hoped not.

Suddenly the two Klingon ships decloaked close to the wormhole. They looked like giant screaming vultures, with their weapons flaring red against the darkness of space. The two Fury ships closest to the wormhole did not return fire right away.

They were surprised.

"Another point for our side," Riker muttered.

He tapped the communications console. This was it. The big moment. Now or never, and all those other clichés.

"Go!" he shouted to Worf and Redbay, feeling absurdly like a soccer coach.

"Aye, sir," Worf said.

"Yes, *sir!*" Redbay said, and Riker could almost see his old friend snap his arm in mock salute. Riker grinned. He might be alone in the shuttle, but he wasn't alone in space. And for some reason having his friend here made him feel more in control.

Worf's shuttle peeled off and headed toward the wormhole.

Redbay followed.

After a moment both opened fire on the two Fury ships, pretending to be making an attack run.

Riker took his ship right in behind him. He forced himself to block out the surrounding fight. His only focus was that wormhole and getting through it.

Nothing else mattered.

Nothing.

"Captain, shields are failing on decks three and ten," Data said.

Picard nodded, then clutched the arm of his chair as the ship rocked from another hit. In front of him a Fury ship exploded, sending an expanding cloud of debris in a circle outward.

"Ensign Eckley, move us closer to the wormhole," he ordered. No matter how much damage, they needed to be close enough to draw the fire away from the shuttles. Worf and Redbay were both making their runs at the Fury ships, adding their firepower to that of the Klingons. Riker's shuttle lagged behind, but was coming in on the same path.

In just seconds, he would be inside the wormhole.

The ship rocked again. The Furies' weapons concentrated on the shields, as they had before. Picard had a feeling that they had encountered this type of protection from some other group. But he bet they were getting a surprise now that the shields were holding.

"The lead ship has sustained serious damage from our torpedoes," Lieutenant Dreod said. She stood in Worf's place at security.

It felt odd not to have his usual bridge complement.

Counselor Troi sat beside him, her face a mask, yet he could feel the tension radiate from her.

No support from that quarter.

Picard stood.

"The damage on decks three and ten has stabilized," Data said. "The shields on the rest of the ship are holding."

The lead Fury ship still stood between them and the wormhole, far too close for Riker's safety.

"Take that lead ship out of there," Picard said.

A barrage of photon torpedoes streaked from the *Enterprise.* They exploded against the shields of the Fury ship. If nothing else, it would get their attention.

Maybe just long enough for Riker to get through.

Worf leaned into his console. His ship weaved through the fire from the Fury ships. He returned the shots with a vigor he hadn't felt in a long, long time.

Worf, son of Mogh, would die with honors. He would die defending his people from the Furies, and serving his ship with pride.

He would give the Furies a fight they would never forget.

The modified shuttlecraft had a great deal of firepower for its size. He used all of it, dodging and weaving, and shooting, all the time making the Furies think he was the most important enemy, diverting their attention from Commander Riker.

The *DoHQay* made a pass at the Fury ship closest to the wormhole. It was circling above, and about to come in for another shot. Worf saw an opening underneath. He swung the shuttle upward, firing continuously as he went.

The Fury ship's shields were failing. Worf focused his fire on where his computer told him their screens were the weakest. The bright red phasers deflected off the shield, leaving a slightly pink glow. Worf was about to use one of his precious photon torpedoes when the Fury ship spun away out of control and exploded.

The explosion was so close that it rocked the shuttle.

Worf clutched the console as he fought for control. He still had fight in him. But the shuttle was swerving dangerously close to the other Fury ship. If Worf didn't get his shuttle turned, he would hit the Fury ship. It would destroy both vessels, but it wouldn't help Commander Riker. He might get caught in the explosion himself.

Worf swerved and barely missed the ship's hull. Sweat dripped off his ridged forehead. But they didn't let him get away that easily.

A phaser blast at close range destroyed his shields.

The shuttle spun away, and Worf had to grip the console to keep from losing his seat.

The screens went dead. The cabin filled with dark smoke, foul-smelling smoke, smoke that came not from an electrical fire, because he knew that smell. No, from something less familiar.

The warp core.

He struggled to regain his shields.

He struggled to regain any vision he could of the fight.

He struggled to bring his weapons on-line.

The air was disappearing from the cabin. Sweat soaked his uniform.

Then he brought the computer on-line.

"Engine failure in ten seconds." The familiar voice started her countdown.

Worf pounded on the console, but nothing else responded.

"Seven . . ."

He couldn't breathe. His chest felt heavy.

"Six . . ."

He ignored it, pushing emergency relays, trying to regain any control at all.

"Five . . ."

The voice sounded so calm. Not even a Klingon would sound that calm in this situation.

"Four . . ."

The smoke was now so thick that he couldn't even see his hands.

"Three . . ."

One glimpse of the battle. Just one. To know if Riker made it.

"Two . . ."

But he would never know. All that he would know was that he had done his best. Mentally he saluted the commander and wished him well.

"One . . ."

Riker had been right. It was a good day to die.

Chapter Twenty-two

THE SHUTTLE WAS ON COURSE. The shuttle *was* on course.

Riker stared at the screen and the console, keeping the wormhole firmly in his vision, ignoring the chaos as best he could.

Eight seconds.

In eight seconds he would be there.

Then Worf's shuttle streaked across space, whipping and spinning like a child's toy thrown by an angry child. Riker glanced at it, feeling suddenly helpless.

Seven seconds.

If he helped Worf, he would jeopardize the entire Federation and his mission.

Six seconds.

Both Klingon ships were firing on the Fury ship

nearest the wormhole. The firefight was incredible, the laser firepower blinding. Redbay had fired a dozen or more shots and then veered away to stay out of the path of the two Birds-of-Prey.

Five seconds.

The *Enterprise* had taken on the main Fury ship in a one-on-one battle. The *Idaho* and the *Madison* were in a three-against-two fight.

Four seconds.

There was no help for Worf. No one could save him. He would die in battle.

"Sorry, old friend," Riker said, wishing Worf could hear him.

But to save Worf would be the worst thing Riker could do. Worf would want to die in battle. It was the best way for a Klingon to die. To make Worf's death meaningful, the mission had to succeed, and it was up to him to make sure it did.

Three seconds. The wormhole suddenly looked huge. The space around it was clear. The other ships had done their jobs.

Two seconds.

Riker glanced at his weapons. The torpedoes were ready. So was he. Worf wouldn't die in vain.

Then, without warning, another Fury ship came out of the mouth of the wormhole directly in front of him.

The ship was huge, and this close, it looked like a demon itself.

He suddenly needed every last ounce of his piloting skill.

He yanked the shuttle hard to port, hoping to flash past the Fury ship before it even had time to react. He was going to be so close that his shuttle would bounce off the Furies' outer screens, he hoped right into the wormhole.

But they saw him.

The ship turned as he did, its larger bulk making the turn shorter. He would make it into the wormhole. They had actually made it easier. . . .

Then a bright flare caught his eye. Point-blank phaser shot.

He didn't even have time to react.

No steering away, no doubling the power of his shields, no time to scream and throw his arms over his head.

One minute he was moving forward, the next his shuttle had turned into a metal fireball, tumbling through space.

"Shields failing," the computer said.

The heat was incredible. The console and chair were both suddenly too hot to touch.

"Environmental controls inoperative," the computer said.

Riker slipped off his tunic jacket, wrapped it around his hand, and hit the stabilizing controls. Somehow he got the shuttle upright, and the screens back on.

Sweat poured from his skin. He had to turn around. He had to get back to that wormhole.

But the Fury ship didn't let up. It followed him, firing as it came.

"Warning. Internal temperature at unsustainable levels," the computer said. "Warning."

"Great," Riker muttered. "Just great."

The heat was even more terrifying considering the

lack of smoke. That meant some sort of severe systems meltdown was imminent.

But it wouldn't take long through that wormhole, if he could just turn around.

"Warning. Systems overload in thirty seconds," the computer said.

He was too far away. He wouldn't make it to the wormhole mouth within a minute, let alone thirty seconds.

Angry, he fired what was left of his phasers at the ship, but it was like firing a water pistol at a three-alarm fire.

He glanced for Worf's shuttle. Maybe, if he couldn't save himself, he could save Worf—but he was too far away.

The Furies hit the shuttle again. The lights flickered on, off, then on again.

"Warning. Shields have failed. Systems overload in fifteen seconds."

He lost his last shields. One more blast and he would be dead.

The console was hot to his wrapped hand. He pounded it with his fist.

"Systems overload in ten seconds."

Ten seconds and no chance of success.

Ten seconds to contemplate the fact that he, William T. Riker, had failed.

The scene on his viewscreens was a nightmare. Redbay had flown thousands of mock space battles while testing ships, but never had he thought he would be a firsthand witness and player in one of the most important battles, with the survival of the Federation and the Klingon Empire at stake.

And the Federation and Klingons were losing.

Worf's shuttle had taken some serious hits and was tumbling out of control. Riker had almost made it when another Fury ship had appeared in front of him, blasting him away from the wormhole like a paper toy in a strong wind.

But luckily, that Fury ship hadn't seen Redbay. Instead it followed Riker, pounding him with shot after shot.

Now Redbay was the only one left.

And the wormhole was there in front of him like a gaping black mouth.

All he had to do was beat any of those Fury ships to it. But Riker's attempt had clued them in. They knew the shuttles weren't escaping, but trying for the wormhole. The Fury ships, fighting with the starships, were actually backing closer to the wormhole.

To guard it.

"Hang in there, buddy," he said aloud as Riker's shuttle took another full blast. "I'll give them something more to think about in just a second."

His hands flew over the controls of the shuttle, keying in a familiar sequence. He'd run a hundred ships through it in test, but never under actual battle circumstances. It was called, among the test pilots, the old "Down and Out" pattern. He had no idea how it got its name, some pilot long before he came along.

The Down and Out consisted of taking a ship at a wide, sweeping, almost lazy arch, then suddenly veering at the target. The theory was that a ship following would be thrown off guard by the move and the ship making the move would gain a slight advantage in distance.

That was the theory, anyway.

He finished the entering the sequence into the computer and engaged.

Around him the battle seemed to flash past as he took the shuttle almost away from the wormhole in a wide arch.

"Three more seconds," he said to himself.

The wormhole was a gaping mouth off his port side.

He waited. Waited. Then said "Now!" as he punched the board hard. The shuttle veered sharply to port, increasing speed to its maximum subwarp. The wormhole grew directly in his front screen, now only a few very long seconds away.

"Right on the money." He could feel himself starting to celebrate another successful move, just as he used to do back at the testing area.

Then he was reminded that this was no longer a test as a blast from below hit the shuttle.

"What?"

It took all his skills and strength just to stay in the pilot's seat. The shuttle was knocked away, and its tumbling momentum took it past the mouth of the wormhole, missing by a large enough distance to make no difference.

A miss was a miss.

The shuttle kept tumbling, and he let it as he searched for a bearing on what had hit him. Even with the shuttle spinning, it didn't take him long to find the problem. One of the Fury ships had veered away from its fight with the Klingons to take him out of his run at the hole. But now the Klingon Bird-of-Prey was stalking it, engaging it again. And from the looks of it, the Klingon ship was winning this time.

For the moment he was safe. He quickly stabilized the tumble of the shuttle and turned it around, going in a wide arch over the battle. First things first. He needed to get back to the correct side of the wormhole.

The mouth side.

"Well, that sure didn't work," he said out loud again. "And I got to stop talking to myself so much. Just as soon as this mission is over."

Sweat dripped from his face as he did a quick check of the systems. His screens were at fifty percent, but otherwise the ship was fine. From the looks of it, he was in a lot better shape than Worf. His shuttle seemed to be completely dead in space.

Redbay took the shuttle at full speed back into a position far above and to one side of the wormhole. It seemed to take forever, but in real time it was less than thirty seconds before he was in place.

From here the battle looked like a bunch of toys fighting. But he knew that in those toys real beings were dying, giving their lives for what they believed.

"Looks like I'm still the only shot. Got to make this one work."

He studied the situation carefully. One of the Fury ships had backed almost to the mouth of the wormhole, but the other Klingon ship was giving it a pounding. The oval shape of the hole looked like a small button against the starfields of space.

A very small target.

Very small.

Suddenly he knew how to get in there. "You better

be as good as you've claimed," he said aloud. "Or you're going to be very, very dead."

He punched in a few quick commands, then glanced at the screen. Riker's shuttle was still tumbling out of control. Will had wanted to see the Redbay Maneuver firsthand. "Well, old friend, you finally get your chance," Redbay said, wishing Will were in the shuttle with him. He didn't want to think about his friend on a damaged shuttle, about to die for nothing.

Redbay would make certain they all succeeded.

He never really was starship material. He had always been a pilot. Only now the tests were done. This was real.

Very real.

The Redbay Maneuver was a test-pilot stunt he'd run many a ship through. In essence it was a ninety-degree turn in space. He used impulse drive to move the ship in one direction. Then, with an almost instantaneous firing and shutting down of the warp drive, he would turn the ship ninety degrees while in the forming and collapsing warp bubble. He'd been the first to try it and make it work; thus he got the honor of the name.

He had three problems. The first was simple. He had never run a shuttlecraft through this particular maneuver.

The second was related to the first: The shuttle's stabilizers would be strained beyond the recommended endurance. If they failed he would be nothing more than a large splash of red on the darkness of space. But the stabilizers would hold. They'd have to. He had no other choice if he wanted to live.

215

And the third was a big problem in and of itself. If he missed the wormhole, he'd be going so fast he'd never make it back into position before the next Fury ship arrived. He'd never have a second chance.

But going fast was a good thing in this situation, because none of the Fury ships would have time to take a shot at him.

So he just wouldn't miss.

It was that simple.

He initiated the procedure, setting the speed at full impulse. Then he aimed the shuttle at a ninety-degree angle across the mouth of the wormhole. It actually would appear that he was heading for the battle between the *Madison,* the *Idaho,* and the three Fury ships. They might even think he was trying to get back to the *Enterprise.*

With only a quick glance at Riker's tumbling ship—it still hadn't righted itself—he focused all his attention on making the turn at exactly the right instant.

"Three."

"Two."

"One."

"Now!" he shouted to the empty shuttle cabin, and triggered the Redbay Maneuver.

The shuttle stabilizers screamed in protest.

But he held on, praying his theories were right.

And all the years of practice would pay off.

Chapter Twenty-three

THE *ENTERPRISE* ROCKED. Picard stood on the bridge, his hands clasped behind his back, presenting, he hoped, a calm in the center of the storm.

Around him, the red-alert lights were flashing. The regular lighting was on three-quarter power, because Mr. La Forge had rerouted the environmental controls to the shields.

So far they were holding.

But Picard didn't know how long they would hold.

The battle raged around the wormhole. He had managed to get the *Enterprise* between the lead Fury ship and the wormhole, providing an opening for the shuttlecrafts.

"Lieutenant Worf's shuttle has been hit," Data said. "It appears to have lost helm control. Life-support is failing."

"Lock on to him, Mr. Data."

"Sir, we cannot beam him out now. We would have to lower our shields."

"I know that, Mr. Data." Picard stared at the screen. The tiny shuttlecraft looked like a bug against the giant Fury ships. "We'll beam him when we can."

"If we wait too long, sir, he—"

"I am aware of the risks, Mr. Data."

Data nodded and swiveled back, facing his console. Troi clasped her hands together. She hadn't gotten out of her chair since the fight started. Picard wasn't sure if she could stand.

She was aware of the risks as well. Most likely neither Worf nor Will Riker would return.

Picard wouldn't lose two good men in a failed mission if he had anything to say about it.

The *Enterprise* rocked again.

"Shields holding," Eckley said.

"Return fire," Picard said.

But as he stared at the screen, he didn't watch his own battle. He watched the shuttlecrafts.

Redbay broke off his run, veering to starboard to give Riker a clear path to the wormhole.

"Another Fury ship is emerging from the wormhole," Data said.

"Warn Commander Riker!" Picard shouted, but it was too late. In horror Picard watched as Riker moved his shuttle in a quick series of moves to a course that would take it speeding past the new Fury ship and into the wormhole.

Only the Fury ship had another plan.

With a phaser burst it sent Riker's shuttle tumbling, then moved after it like a bully chasing a small victim.

"Move to intercept that new ship," Picard ordered.

The deck rocked from the impact of a phaser blast from the one ship they already were fighting.

"Shields failing on decks fifteen through twenty," Data said.

"Mr. La Forge," Picard said to the air in front of him. "Can you give me an uninterrupted phaser blast, sustained for three seconds?"

"Yes, sir." La Forge's voice sounded strong and confident. "But the shot will be a drain."

"Then drain us, Mr. La Forge," Picard ordered.

"Aye, sir."

Picard turned to tactical. "Lieutenant Dreod, target that new ship with a three-second laser shot at full intensity."

The young lieutenant nodded. "Ready."

Picard turned to look at the screen. If the Furies had tried to interrupt the *Enterprise* shields by varying the modulation, then their ships must use the same type of modulating shield. A sustained blast to that type of shield should bring it down.

The new ship was moving slowly after Riker's shuttle. Will might already be dead in there, but those Furies were going to pay the price for killing his first officer. "Fire!"

The laser blast seemed to last for an eternity. And before it had ended, the shields of the Fury ship had gone from blue to a bright red and then disappeared. The ship exploded like a kid's balloon stuck by a pin.

Picard felt no joy. No happiness.

Riker was too far from the wormhole. Even if he turned around, he probably didn't have a chance. Picard could see that without looking at the readings.

The mission had failed.

Picard hoped the other captains had an idea, because he was all out.

The other Fury ship had backed off slightly.

"Sir," Data said. "Lieutenant Redbay's shuttle is moving on an arching course over the wormhole."

Picard turned to the screen. The shuttle was moving at a arching angle almost away from the wormhole.

Why would he do that? He wasn't even close to the target. "What is he doing?" Picard said softly.

"Perhaps he's trying something, sir," Eckley said.

"He is out there. He might see something we don't." Troi sounded tired. She knew it was all lost as well.

Suddenly the shuttle veered sharply and gained speed at the wormhole.

"He is trying a training pilot's stunt called a Down and Out," Data said. "It might work."

But Picard could tell almost instantly that Data had spoken too soon. The Fury ship closest to the wormhole broke away from the Klingon Bird-of-Prey and hit the shuttle with a direct shot.

Redbay went spinning off course and past the wormhole.

The silence on the bridge felt like a smothering blanket. Picard wanted to order the air-filtration system turned up. More than that, he wanted to be anywhere but here. Maybe back in France, sitting on top of a hill with a gentle breeze blowing over his face.

But unless they stopped the Furies here, that might never be possible again. For him or for anyone else.

He turned to Data. "Inform the *Madison* and the

Idaho that they need to launch their shuttles. Make sure they have all the details."

"Yes, sir," Data said, and his fingers danced over his board, sending off his messages.

The *Enterprise* rocked again with the hit of another Fury blast.

"Shields are still holding," Lieutenant Dreod said.

"Good," Picard said, forcing his attention back on the main screen and the battle in front of him. Maybe, just maybe, they could hold on long enough to get one of the other starships' shuttles through. It was possible.

Another Fury ship appeared from the wormhole and moved immediately into the fight with the Klingons.

"Message sent, sir," Data said. "And Lieutenant Redbay has recovered and is moving into a position high above the wormhole."

"What?" Picard said. He turned and stared at the main screen showing the wormhole and the battle. Sure enough, Redbay's shuttle was a large distance above and to the port side of the wormhole.

"He's holding position," Data said.

"Maybe he's injured," Eckley said.

"I show his shields at fifty percent," Data said, "and all other systems on the shuttle functioning normally."

On the screen the shuttle started to move, not at the wormhole, but more in the direction of the *Idaho* and the *Madison*.

Picard made himself stand and stare, not believing that an officer on his ship would not continue to try to carry out his duty. But it looked as if Lieutenant

Redbay was retreating, right at a time when the Federation needed him the most.

Suddenly the shuttle seemed to stop in flight.

The colors of the rainbow flashed, indicating the shuttle had gone into warp. But it was only a flash, and the next instant the shuttle was streaking toward the wormhole.

And then the shuttle was gone.

Into the mouth of the wormhole.

"The Redbay Maneuver!" Eckley shouted in an excited voice. "He pulled off the Redbay Maneuver."

"The shuttle has entered the wormhole," Data said, confirming what Picard had just seen.

One of their shuttles had gone through.

He glanced at Troi. She stood slowly, keeping one hand on the chair for balance. She was weak, but Redbay's action seemed to give her strength.

Picard let out a breath. So Redbay hadn't been running at all. He'd just been outsmarting them all.

Maybe this death wasn't all for nothing.

If the lieutenant knew what to do.

If, if, if.

Redbay felt as if he were sliding down a stair railing in a thick smoke cloud while everyone else was climbing slowly upward. "Weird," he said aloud. "Really weird."

His sensors showed that he was passing over a hundred Fury ships stacked up in the wormhole. The Federation would have no chance if all these ships made it through. It was his job to make sure they didn't.

The inside of the wormhole was nothing like they

described the wormhole at *Deep Space Nine* to be. This one swirled gray and black, with the line of Fury ships being nothing more than hulking shadows streaking past.

Then, almost as quickly as it started, he was back in real space.

He did a quick scan. The power source was right where Will said it would be. It seemed like a small asteroid hanging in the blackness of space, right at the mouth of the wormhole. But it was actually a huge machine, with power flowing at it from twenty different directions.

"Impressive," Redbay said aloud.

A line of Fury ships seemed to stretch off into the distance, slowly making their way into the wormhole. Redbay didn't even think about glancing at how many there were. Just one was more than a match for this shuttle. The rest didn't matter.

For the moment they didn't react to his sudden appearance. But that would last for only a moment. He'd only get one shot, so he better make it quick and right.

He dove the shuttle right at the small asteroid-like machine, quickly finding the spot Will had said was the target.

"Deep breath," Redbay said aloud to the empty cabin. "This is just another test run. Make it happen."

He locked three torpedoes on target and fired them in quick succession at the machine.

The closest Fury ship broke out of line and headed his way, firing as it came. The shields of the shuttle held, but they wouldn't for long.

Redbay took the shuttle into a steep climb away

from the asteroid as the huge machine started to glow red.

Then a tremendous explosion sent the shuttlecraft spinning like a dry leaf in a strong wind.

"Got it," he said, laughing. "I got it!"

He fought to regain control of the shuttle, but without luck. The blast had completely destroyed all his controls.

"Warning. Internal stabilizers failing," the computer voice said.

"Oh, just great," Redbay said as the increasing forces pinned him into his chair.

With a snap the shuttle's internal stabilizers failed, smashing him against the inside wall of the shuttle and sending him into blackness.

Between the *Idaho* and the *Madison*, a Fury ship exploded. Another Fury ship seemed to be nothing more than a dead hulk. The remaining ships turned to the wormhole, but both Klingon ships moved into their paths and began firing.

Another ship appeared at the mouth of the wormhole.

Picard felt his shoulders sink. Redbay's shuttle must have been destroyed going through.

"Sir," Data said. "The wormhole is collapsing."

Picard couldn't see it. The new Fury ship seemed about to come through.

Then it seemed to elongate. He could almost hear the screams of the Furies inside.

The wormhole stretched, then shrank, then winked out as if it had never been, taking the ship with it.

The bridge broke into wild cheering.

"Redbay found his target," Picard said, his voice soft. He wanted to cheer with the others on the bridge, but something inside kept him silent.

He glanced at the ruined shuttles. "Shields down, Mr. Data. Transporter room, beam Lieutenant Worf aboard."

"Sir," Data said. "It is too late—"

"Anderson, beam him directly to sickbay."

"Aye, sir."

"Sir," Data said, his voice soft, "Commander Riker is still alive."

Picard whirled. "Transporter, get a lock on commander Riker and get him out of there. Now."

A moment later Picard heard, "Done, sir. He's here."

"And Lieutenant Worf?"

"We beamed his body into sickbay, sir."

His body. Two officers down. One survived. It was too soon to feel anything.

The battle wasn't done yet.

Picard turned and stared at the screen. "Screens back up. Open a hailing channel to the main Fury ship."

"Done, sir," Lieutenant Dreod said.

On the main monitor, the screen flickered and then the Furies' leader appeared. Its scarlet skin was peeling. The air around it looked clean, but the back of its chair was coated in creatures.

Dead creatures.

Thousands and thousands of tiny bugs.

The mucus around its mouth was white. Its eyes were yellow. Several dead crew appeared on the screen behind it.

"We have closed your wormhole," Picard said. "You are outnumbered and outgunned."

"I am aware of the situation, Picard," the Fury said, its voice raspy as if it were in pain.

"If you surrender, it will be as if we had never fought. We will . . ."

"Talk, talk, talk. I suppose if I turn my ship over to you, you will want to talk about it." The Fury raised a hand. Long ropes of scarlet flesh hung from it, and a black ichor covered the lower part of the palm. "You talk, but you do not listen, Picard."

"I am listening now."

"I told you we do not bargain. We conquer."

"That seems unlikely today," Picard said.

"That it does," the creature said. "So if you would be so kind as to place our souls with those of our brothers from the *Rath,* we will go now. But there will be a tomorrow. On that you can count."

The creature laughed a sour laugh. "But I'm afraid I will not discuss it with you. Sweet dreams."

The creature smiled. The mucus dripped down its chin, and its yellow eyes had a crazed look.

A chill ran through Picard. A chill that had nothing to do with fear rays or heightened senses. Only a race memory generations old.

Picard would see that face in his dreams.

He knew that, and the creature knew that.

And neither one of them would forget it.

Then the screen went black, replaced a moment later by the view of the Fury ship.

It exploded.

As Picard knew it would.

The other two remaining Fury ships did the same almost instantly.

"That makes no sense," Eckley said. "They didn't need to die."

"Yes, they did," Troi said. "They were afraid."

Picard turned to her. She was swaying slightly as she stood. "Of what, Counselor? Us?"

"Captain," she said, "as victorious demons they were all-powerful. As prisoners of war, they were merely creatures from another quadrant defeated."

"They died for an illusion?" he said, not quite able to believe it.

She shook her head. "They died because of the future that one mentioned," she said. "They died because they knew someday, their people will try again."

Picard shuddered, glancing at the debris-filled blackness. And out there he knew were pods full of small dolls. Poppets full of the souls of those in the ships, to be placed with those from the *Rath,* to wait until the next time.

"They'll be back," Troi said.

He nodded. Safe far across the galaxy, they would lick their wounds, and heal. They would be back, stronger than they had been before.

Chapter Twenty-four

LIEUTENANT BOBBY YOUNG still clung to life. His face was yellow with strain, but his eyes were clear. He knew that he was on the *Enterprise* and the ship was fighting a battle with the Furies.

Beverly Crusher believed that if the *Enterprise* lost the battle, Lieutenant Young would lose his mind.

But if the Furies were defeated, Young would recover. He might never serve in Starfleet again, but he would be able to ski. She knew he loved skiing. When she had asked him to name the most important thing in his life, he had finally spoken. One word, whispered like a lover's name.

Skiing.

And now it looked like he would be able to go. The wormhole was destroyed. The Fury ships had exploded, and the Federation was saved.

At great cost.

Commander Riker and Lieutenant Worf. She had shut off the display when she heard that.

"Doctor," one of her assistants cried. "We're going to be getting wounded."

Beverly pulled herself out of the chair beside Lieutenant Young's bed. "Get the beds ready, pronto. Have the standby team ready."

This was what she had prepared for early in the mission, and it was finally happening.

A body made up of particles of light flickered above the main bed. It was long and broad and—

Klingon.

Worf!

His eyes were open, but unseeing. His ridged forehead was covered with black stains, and burns showed through his uniform.

He wasn't breathing.

But he was here.

At least he was here.

She bent over him. She would save him. She had to save him. She would rescue one of their team, even if Riker was gone.

"All right, everyone," she shouted. "Get his heart and lungs working, stat. We don't know how long he's been gone."

She glanced at the diagnostic. His heart wasn't working. He wasn't breathing. The smoke, according to the medical tricorder, had been a deadly mixture of chemicals from the shuttle's engine. His lungs had collapsed.

If she had to estimate how long he was gone, she would guess a good twenty-five minutes. And even if she could bring him back, she might not be able to spare him brain damage.

Behind her the door whooshed open and Deanna came in. She immediately took Worf's hand and held it. Then she looked up at Beverly, who shook her head.

"Anything," Deanna said. "Try anything."

Beverly glanced at the overhead readings. Worf's hearts and lungs seemed to be clear now and his blood had cycled a few times, cleaning out the poisons. But there was no brain activity. The only chance he had was to be shocked back.

She quickly prepared an extra-sized dose of Klaxtal, the strongest stimulant she knew of that would work on Klingons.

She glanced at Deanna, who was staring down at Worf's smudged face. "Stand back," Beverly said. "This might cause some sharp muscle contractions."

Deanna stood back, but didn't release Worf's hand.

Beverly injected the Klaxtal and then moved out of the way. She had seen Klingons break human doctors' limbs while under the influence of this drug.

But Worf didn't move.

Deanna glanced at her. Beverly was about to step in to try again when Worf's powerful body jerked upward, his legs kicking, his arms flailing. Deanna let go and the two of them watched as Worf's body twitched and bucked, then lay still.

Very still.

It hadn't worked. Beverly stepped back up beside Worf. "Worf, damn you," she said. "Come back to—"

Suddenly the monitor over Worf blinked, and the next instant he took a huge, shuddering breath.

"He's back," Deanna said, moving up beside him and touching his head.

But the question was whether or not he was completely back.

Beverly glanced at the reading. There was brain function, but she couldn't tell if there was damage.

"Worf," she said. "Worf. You need to speak to me."

He still didn't open his eyes.

"Deanna," she said.

Deanna nodded, then bent over him, her hair hiding his face. "Worf," she said. "Please—"

His right hand went to her throat. "I will not talk!" he said.

"Worf," Beverly said. "It's Deanna!"

He let go and she staggered backward, smiling. "Deanna?" he said. "I am on the *Enterprise?*"

"Yes," Beverly said. She glanced at the scan beside the bed. His conscious brain functions gave a better reading. He would be all right.

"The Furies?"

"Are defeated," Deanna said, her voice rasping.

"And Commander Riker?"

"Is fine," Deanna said. "But he insisted on going to the bridge before coming here, even though both his hands are burnt."

Beverly glanced at her. She hadn't heard that Riker lived.

Deanna smiled, never taking her eyes from Worf "The captain should be ordering him here any minute."

But something in Deanna's eyes said that wasn't the whole story. Beverly caught the look, but Worf appeared too tired to care. "My head feels as if it has been trampled by a herd of Klingon wildebeests," he said.

Beverly smiled at him, and took her place beside him. "Your head is hard, and that probably saved your life," she said. "But I do need to check the rest of your injuries. And I need to tell the captain that you're all right."

"I will," Deanna said. "He'll be very pleased to hear it."

Several hours later, Picard sank into a chair in Ten-Forward. Commander Will Riker already had a seat at the table. He was staring out the window, at the stars streaking past. His hands were wrapped in light bandages, and his eyes had deep shadows. It looked as if he had lost weight in the last day, and maybe, just maybe, he had.

Guinan came over, a carafe filled with purple liquid in her right hand, two snifters in her left.

"Tea for me, Guinan," Picard said.

She grinned. "I've been saving this Nestafarian brandy for a special occasion. I think defeating the Furies counts, don't you?"

"I don't feel like celebrating," Riker said, his gaze still on the stars.

"I don't think special occasions are always celebrations," Guinan said. She put the brandy down between them, poured a centimeter of purple liquid into the bottom of each glass, and pushed them toward her customers. "Sometimes special occasions are the quiet moments when healing can begin."

She got up, and left them. Picard watched her go. He relied on her wisdom and her strength. She was letting him know that she approved of his action, of the path he had chosen to defeat his fears, and the Furies, all at the same time.

But he didn't approve. He didn't feel as if he'd done enough. He wasn't certain the wormhole was closed forever. And he had lost what promised to be one of Starfleet's top new officers.

Riker held out his bandaged hands. Picard had never seen anything quite like that before.

"Dr. Crusher doesn't trust me not to tear off the new skin," Riker said. "So she bandaged me."

"You're off duty, Number One. You can rest, you know."

Riker nodded. He glanced at the stars. "But I have some practicing to do," he said softly, almost to himself. "Flying old atmospheric jets in a holodeck program. I have a rematch scheduled. Someday."

Picard finally understood. Redbay. They were both thinking of the lieutenant, alone on the other side of the wormhole.

With the Furies.

A sacrifice either one of them would have gladly made in his stead. A sacrifice Riker was supposed to make, but circumstances prevented.

In some ways, it was just as hard on this end, knowing that they would never know how—or if— Redbay survived. They only knew that he had done his job.

Now they had to go on. When they had signed up for Starfleet, they knew the risks.

One of those risks was the loss of their own lives.

The other, harder risk, was losing friends.

Picard picked up his snifter, twirled the brandy, and inhaled. It had a spicy, dark scent. "Tell me about Lieutenant Redbay, Will," Picard said.

Riker stared at Picard for a moment, then took a brandy snifter in one bandaged hand.

"Not the lieutenant I can read about in the records," Picard said. "I want to know the man."

Riker nodded, taking a sip. "Lieutenant Redbay?" He glanced out at the stars for a moment, then went on. "Lieutenant *Sam* Redbay was my friend."

He lifted his brandy snifter in a silent toast.

Picard joined him.

The
Invasion
Continues
In

STAR TREK
DEEP SPACE NINE®
Invasion!

BOOK THREE

Time's Enemy

by

L. A. Graf

"It looks like they're preparing for an invasion," Jadzia Dax said.

Sisko grunted, gazing out at the expanse of dark-crusted cometary ice that formed the natural hull of Starbase 1. Above the curving ice horizon, the blackness of Earth's Oort cloud should have glittered with bright stars and the barely brighter glow of the distant sun. Instead, what it glittered with were the docking lights of a dozen short-range attack ships—older and more angular versions of the *Defiant*—as well as the looming bulk of two Galaxy-class starships, the *Mukaikubo* and the *Breedlove*. One glance had told Sisko that such a gathering of force couldn't have been the random result of ship refittings and shore leaves. Starfleet was preparing for a major encounter with someone. He just wished he knew who.

"I thought we came here to deal with a *non*military emergency." In the sweep of transparent aluminum windows, Sisko could see Julian Bashir's dark reflection glance up from the chair he'd sprawled in after an uninterested glance at the view. Beyond the doctor, the huge conference room was as empty as it had been ten minutes ago when they'd first been escorted into it. "Otherwise, wouldn't Admiral Hayman have asked us to come in the *Defiant* instead of a high-speed courier?"

Sisko snorted. "Admirals never *ask* anything, Doctor. And they never tell you any more than you need to know to carry out their orders efficiently."

"Especially this admiral," Dax added, an unexpected note of humor creeping into her voice. Sisko raised an eyebrow at her, then heard a gravelly snort and the simultaneous hiss of the conference-room door opening. He swung around to see a rangy, long-boned figure in ordinary Starfleet coveralls crossing the room toward them. Dax surprised him by promptly stepping forward, hands outstretched in welcome.

"How have you been, Judith?"

"Promoted." The silver-haired woman's angular face lit with something approaching a sparkle. "It almost makes up for getting this old." She clasped Dax's hands warmly for a moment, then turned her attention to Sisko. "So this is the Benjamin Sisko Curzon told me so much about. It's a pleasure to finally meet you, Captain."

Sisko slanted a wary glance at his science officer. "Um—likewise, I'm sure. Dax?"

The Trill cleared her throat. "Benjamin, allow me to introduce you to Rear Admiral Judith Hayman. She and I—well, she and Curzon, actually—got to know each other on Vulcan during the Klingon peace negotiations several years ago. Judith, this is Captain Benjamin Sisko of *Deep Space Nine,* and our station's chief medical officer, Dr. Julian Bashir."

"Admiral." Bashir nodded crisply.

"Our orders said this was a Priority One Emergency," Sisko reminded his superior officer almost as soon as she released his hand. "I assume that means whatever you brought us here to do is urgent."

Hayman's strong face lost its smile. "Possibly," she said. "Although perhaps not urgent in the way we usually think of it."

Sisko scowled. "Forgive my bluntness, Admiral, but I've been dragged from my command station without explanation, ordered not to use my own ship under any circumstances, brought to the oldest and least useful starbase in the Federation"—he made a gesture of reined-in impatience at the bleak cometary landscape outside the windows—"and you're telling me you're not sure how *urgent* this problem is?"

"No one is sure, Captain. That's part of the reason we brought you here." The admiral's voice chilled into something between grimness and exasperation. "What we *are* sure of is that we could be facing potential disaster." She reached into the front pocket of her coveralls and tossed two ordinary-looking data chips onto the conference table. "The first thing I need you and your medical officer to do is review these data records."

"Data records," Sisko repeated, trying for the non-committal tone he'd perfected over years of trying to deal with the equally high-handed and inexplicable behavior of Kai Winn.

"Admiral, forgive us, but we assumed this actually *was* an emergency," Julian Bashir explained, in such polite bafflement that Sisko guessed he must be emulating Garak's unctuous demeanor. "If so, we could have reviewed your data records ten hours ago. All you had to do was send them to *Deep Space Nine* through subspace channels."

"Too dangerous, even using our most secure codes." The bleak certainty in Hayman's voice made Sisko blink in surprise. "And if you were listening, young man, you'd have noticed that I said this was the *first* thing I needed you to do. Now, would you please sit down, Captain?"

He took the place she indicated at one of the conference table's inset data stations, then waited while she settled Bashir at the station on the opposite side. He noticed she made no attempt to seat Dax, although there were other empty stations available.

"This review procedure is not a standard one," Hayman said, without further preliminaries. "As a control on the validity of some data we've recently received, we're going to ask you to examine ship's logs and medical records without knowing their origin. We'd like your analysis of them. Computer, start data-review programs Sisko-One and Bashir-One."

Sisko's monitor flashed to life, not with pictures but with a thick ribbon of multilayered symbols and abbreviated words, slowly scrolling from left to right. He stared at it for a long, blank moment before a whisper of memory turned it familiar instead of alien. One of the things Starfleet Academy asked cadets to do was determine the last three days of a starship's voyage when its main computer memory had failed. The solution was to reconstruct computer records from each of the ship's individual system buffers— records that looked exactly like these.

"These are multiple logs of buffer output from individual ship systems, written in standard Starfleet machine code," he said. Dax made an interested noise and came to stand behind him. "It looks like someone downloaded the last commands given to life-support, shields, helm, and phaser-bank control. There's another system here, too, but I can't identify it."

"Photon-torpedo control?" Dax suggested, leaning over his shoulder to scrutinize it.

"I don't think so. It might be a sensor buffer." Sisko scanned the lines of code intently while they scrolled by. He could recognize more of the symbols now, although most of the abbreviations on the fifth line still baffled him. "There's no sign of navigations, either—the command buffers in those systems may have been destroyed by whatever took out the ship's main computer." Sisko grunted as four of the five logs recorded wild fluctuations and then degenerated into solid black lines. "And there goes everything else. Whatever hit this ship crippled it beyond repair."

Dax nodded. "It looks like some kind of EM pulse took out all of the ship's circuits—everything lost power except for life-support, and that had to switch to auxiliary circuits." She glanced up at the admiral. "Is that all the record we have, Admiral? Just those few minutes?"

"It's all the record we *trust,*" Hayman said enigmatically. "There are some visual bridge logs that I'll show you in a minute, but those could have been tampered with. We're fairly sure the buffer outputs weren't." She glanced up at Bashir, whose usual restless energy had focused down to a silent intensity of concentration on his own data screen. "The medical logs we found were much more extensive. You have time to review the buffer outputs again, if you'd like."

"Please," Sisko and Dax said in unison.

"Computer, repeat data program Sisko-One."

Machine code crawled across the screen again, and this time Sisko stopped trying to identify the individual symbols in it. He vaguely remembered one of his Academy professors saying that reconstructing a starship's movements from the individual buffer outputs of its systems was a lot like reading a symphony score. The trick was not to analyze each line individually, but to get a sense of how all of them were functioning in tandem.

"This ship was in a battle," he said at last. "But I think it was trying to escape, not fight. The phaser banks all show discharge immediately after power fluctuations are recorded for the shields."

"Defensive action," Dax agreed, and pointed at the screen. "And look at how much power they had to divert from life-support to keep the shields going. Whatever was after them was big."

"They're trying some evasive actions now—" Sisko broke off, seeing something he'd missed the first time in that mysterious fifth line of code. Something that froze his stomach. It was the same Romulan symbol that appeared on his command board every time the cloaking device was engaged on the *Defiant*.

"This was a cloaked Starfleet vessel!" He swung around to fix the admiral with a fierce look. "My understanding was that only the *Defiant* had been sanctioned to carry a Romulan cloaking device!"

Hayman met his stare without a ripple showing in her calm competence. "I can assure you that Starfleet isn't running any unauthorized cloaking devices. Watch the log again, Captain Sisko."

He swung back to his monitor. "Computer, rerun data program Sisko-One at one-quarter speed," he said. The five concurrent logs crawled across the screen in slow motion, and this time Sisko focused on the coordinated interactions between the helm and the phaser banks. If he had any hope of identifying the class and generation of this starship, it would be from the tactical maneuvers it could perform.

"Time the helm changes versus the phaser bursts," Dax suggested from behind him in an unusually quiet voice. Sisko wondered if she was beginning to harbor the same ominous suspicion he was.

"I know." For the past hundred years, the speed of helm shift versus the speed of phaser refocus had been the basic determining factor of battle tactics. Sisko's gaze flickered from top line to third, counting off milliseconds by the ticks along the edge of the data record. The phaser refocus rates he found were startlingly fast, but far more chilling was the almost instantaneous response of this starship's helm in its tactical runs. There was only one ship he knew of that had the kind of overpowered warp engines needed to bring it so dangerously close to the edge of survivable maneuvers. And there was only one commander who had used his spare time to perfect the art of skimming along the edge of that envelope, the way the logs told him this ship's commander had done.

This time when Sisko swung around to confront Judith Hayman, his concern had condensed into cold, sure knowledge. "Where did you find these records, Admiral?"

She shook her head. "Your analysis first, Captain. I need your unbiased opinion before I answer any questions or show you the visual logs. Otherwise, we'll never know for sure if these data can be trusted."

Sisko blew out a breath, trying to find words for conclusions he wasn't even sure he believed. "This ship—it wasn't just cloaked like the *Defiant*. It actually *was* the *Defiant*." He heard Dax's indrawn breath. "And when it was destroyed in battle, the man commanding it was me."

The advantage of having several lifetimes of experience to draw on, Jadzia Dax often thought, was that there wasn't much left in the universe that could surprise you. The disadvantage was that you no longer remembered how to cope with surprise. In particular, she'd forgotten the sensation of facing a reality so improbable that logic insisted it could not exist while all your senses told you it did.

Like finding out that the mechanical death throes you had just seen were those of your very own starship.

"Thank you, Captain Sisko," Admiral Hayman said. "That confirms what we suspected."

"But how can it?" Dax straightened to frown at the older woman. "Admiral, if these records are real and not computer constructs—then they must have somehow come from our future!"

"Or from an alternate reality," Sisko pointed out. He swung the chair of his data station around with the kind of controlled force he usually reserved for the command chair of the *Defiant*. "Just where in space were these transmissions picked up, Admiral?"

Hayman's mouth quirked, an expression Jadzia found unreadable but which Curzon's memories interpreted as rueful. "They weren't—at least not as transmissions. What you're seeing there, Captain, are—"

"—actual records."

It took Dax a moment to realize that those unexpected words had been spoken by Julian Bashir. The elegant human accent was unmistakably his, but the grim tone was not.

"What are you talking about, Doctor?" Sisko demanded.

"These are actual records, taken directly from the *Defiant*." From here, all Dax could see of him was the intent curve of his head and neck as he leaned over his data station. "Medical logs in my own style, made for my own personal use. There's no reason to transmit medical data in this form."

The unfamiliar numbness of surprise was fading at last, and Dax found it replaced by an equally strong curiosity. She skirted the table to join him. "What kind of medical data are they, Julian?"

He threw her a startled upward glance, almost as if he'd forgotten she was there, then scrambled out of his chair to face her. "Confidential patient records," he said, blocking her view of the screen. "I don't think you should see them."

The Dax symbiont might have accepted that explanation, but Jadzia knew the young human doctor too well. The troubled expression on his face wasn't put there by professional ethics. "Are they my records?" she asked, then patted his arm when he winced. "I expected you to find them, Julian. If this was our *Defiant,* then we were probably all on it when it was— I mean, when it *will be*—destroyed."

"What I don't understand," Sisko said with crisp impatience, "is how we can have actual records preserved from an event that hasn't happened yet."

Admiral Hayman snorted. "No one understands that, Captain Sisko—which is why Starfleet Command thought this might be an elaborate forgery." Her piercing gaze slid to Bashir. "Doctor, are you convinced that the man who wrote those medical logs was a *future* you? They're not pastiches put together from bits and pieces of your old records, in order to fool us?"

Bashir shook his head, vehemently. "What these medical logs say that I did—no past records of mine could have been altered enough to mimic that. They have to have been written by a future me." He gave Dax another distressed look. "Although it's a future that I hope to hell never comes true."

"That's a wish the entire Federation is going to share, now that we know these records are genuine."

Hayman thumped herself into the head chair at the conference table, and touched the control panel in front of it. One of the windows on the opposite wall obediently blanked into a viewscreen. "Let me show you why."

The screen flickered blue and then condensed into a familiar wide-screen scan of the *Defiant*'s bridge. It was the viewing angle Dax had gotten used to watching in post-mission analyses, the one recorded by the official logging sensor at the back of the deck. In this frozen still picture, she could see the outline of Sisko's shoulders and head above the back of his chair, and the top of her own head beyond him, at the helm. The *Defiant*'s viewscreen showed darkness spattered with distant fires that looked a little too large and bright to be stars. The edges of the picture were frayed and spangled with blank blue patches, obscuring the figures at the weapons and engineering consoles. Dax thought she could just catch the flash of Kira's earring through the static.

"The record's even worse than it looks here," Hayman said bluntly. "What you're seeing is a computer reconstruction of the scattered bytes we managed to download from the sensor's memory buffer. All we've got is the five-minute run it recorded just before the bridge lost power. Any record it dumped to the main computer before that was lost."

Sisko nodded, acknowledging the warning buried in her dry words. "So we're going to see the *Defiant*'s final battle."

"That's right." Hayman tapped at her control panel again, and the conference room filled with the sound of Kira's tense voice.

"Three alien vessels coming up fast on vector oh-nine-seven. We can't outrun them." The fires on the viewscreen blossomed into the unmistakable red-orange explosions of warp cores breaching under attack. Dax tried to count them, but there were too many, scattered over too wide a sector of space to keep track of. Her stomach roiled in fierce and utter disbelief. How could so many starships be destroyed this quickly? Had all of Starfleet rallied to fight this hopeless future battle?

"They're also moving too fast to track with our quantum torpedoes." The sound of her own voice coming from the image startled her. It sounded impossibly calm to Dax under the circumstances. She saw her future self glance up at the carnage on the viewscreen, but from the back there was no way to tell what she thought of it. "Our course change didn't throw them off. They must be tracking our thermal output."

"Drop cloak." The toneless curtness of Sisko's recorded voice told Dax just how grim the situation must be. "Divert all power to shields and phasers."

The sensor image flickered blue and silent for a moment as a power surge ran through it, then returned to its normal tattered state. Now, however, there were three distinct patches of blue looming closer on the future *Defiant*'s viewscreen.

"What's that?" Bashir asked Hayman, pointing.

The admiral grunted and froze the image while she answered him. "That's the computer's way of saying it couldn't match a known image to the visual bytes it got there."

"The three alien spaceships," Dax guessed. "They're not Klingon or Romulan then."

"Or Cardassian or Jem'Hadar," Bashir added quietly.

"As far as we can tell, they don't match any known spacefaring ship design," Hayman said. "That's what worries us."

Sisko leaned both elbows on the table, frowning at the stilled image intently. "You think we're going be attacked by some unknown force from the Gamma Quadrant?"

"Or worse." The admiral cleared her throat, as if her dramatic words had embarrassed her. "You may have heard rumors about the alien invaders that Captain Picard and the *Enterprise* drove off from Brundage Station. From the spectrum of the energy discharges you're going to see when the alien ships fire their phasers at you, the computer thinks there's more than a slight chance that this could be another invasion force."

Dax repressed a shiver at this casual discussion of their catastrophic future. "You think the *Defiant* is going to be destroyed in a future battle with the Furies?"

"We know they think that this region of space once

belonged to them," Hayman said crisply. "We know they want it back. And we know we didn't destroy their entire fleet in our last encounter, just the artificial wormhole they used to transport themselves to Furies Point. Given the *Defiant*'s posting near the Bajoran wormhole—" She broke off, waving a hand irritably at the screen. "I'm getting ahead of myself. Watch the rest of the visual log first, then I'll answer your questions." Her mouth jerked downward at one corner. "If I can."

She touched the control panel again to resume the log playback. Almost immediately, the viewscreen flashed with a blast of unusually intense phaser fire.

"Damage to forward shield generators," reported O'Brien's tense voice. "Diverting power from rear shield generators to compensate."

"Return fire!" Sisko's computer-reconstructed figure blurred as he leapt from his captain's chair and went to join Dax at the helm. "Starting evasive maneuvers, program delta!"

More flashes screamed across the viewscreen, obscuring the random jerks and wiggles that the stars made during warp-speed maneuvers. The phaser fire washed the *Defiant*'s bridge in such fierce white light that the crew turned into darkly burned silhouettes. An uneasy feeling grew in Dax that she was watching ghosts rather than real people, and she began to understand Starfleet's reluctance to trust that this log was real.

"Evasive maneuvers aren't working!" Kira sounded both fierce and frustrated. "They're firing in all directions, not just at us."

"Their present course vector will take them past us in twelve seconds, point-blank range," Dax warned. "Eleven, ten, nine . . ."

"Forward shields failing!" shouted O'Brien. Behind his voice the ship echoed with the thunderous sound of vacuum breach. "We've lost sectors seventeen and twenty-one—"

"Six, five, four . . ."

"Spin the ship to get maximum coverage from rear shields," Sisko ordered curtly. *"Now!"*

"Two, one . . ."

Another hull breach thundered through the ship, this one louder and closer than before. The sensor image washed blue and silent again with another power surge. Dax held her breath, expecting the black fade of ship destruction to follow it. To her amazement, however, the blue rippled and condensed back into the familiar unbreached contours of the bridge. Emergency lights glowed at each station, making the crew look shadowy and even more unreal.

"Damage reports," Sisko ordered.

"Hull breaches in all sectors below fifteen," O'Brien said grimly. "We've lost the port nacelle, too, Captain."

"Alien ships are veering off at vector five-sixteen point nine." Kira sounded suspicious and surprised in equal measures. Her silhouette turned at the weapons console, earring glittering. "Sensors report they're still firing phasers in all directions. And for some reason, their shields appear to be failing." A distant red starburst lit the viewscreen, followed by two more. "Captain, you're not going to believe this, but it looks like they just blew up!"

Dax saw herself turn to look at Kira, and for the first time caught a dim glimpse of her own features. As far as she could tell, they looked identical to the ones she'd seen in the mirror that morning. Whatever this future was, it wasn't far away.

"Maybe our phasers caused as much damage as theirs did," she suggested hopefully. "Or more."

"I don't think so." O'Brien's voice was even grimmer now. "I've been trying to put our rear shields back on-line, but something's not right. Something's draining them from the outside." His voice scaled upward in disbelief. "Our main core power's being sucked out right through the shield generators!"

"A new kind of weapon?" Sisko demanded. "Something we can neutralize with our phasers?"

The chief engineer made a startled noise. "No, it's not an energy beam at all. It looks more like—"

At that point, with a suddenness that made Dax's stomach clench, the entire viewscreen went dead. She felt her shoulder and hand muscles tense in involuntary protest, and heard Bashir stir uncomfortably beside her. Sisko cursed beneath his breath.

"I know," Admiral Hayman said dryly. "The main circuits picked the worst possible time to give out. That's all the information we have."

"No, it's not." Julian Bashir's voice sounded bleak rather than satisfied, and Dax suspected he would rather not have had the additional information to give them. "I haven't had a chance to read the majority of these medical logs, but I have found the ones that deal with the aftermath of the battle."

Hayman's startled look at him contained a great deal more respect than it had a few moments before, Dax noticed. "There were logs that talked about the battle? No one else noticed that."

"That's because no one else knows my personal abbreviations for the names of the crew," Bashir said simply. "I scanned the records for the ones I thought might have been aboard on this trip. Of the six regular crew, Odo wasn't mentioned anywhere. I'm guessing he stayed back on *Deep Space Nine*. My records for Kira and O'Brien indicate they were lost in some kind of shipboard battle, trying to ward off an invading force. Sisko seems to have been injured then and to have died afterward, but I'm not sure exactly when. And Dax—" He stopped to clear his throat and then resumed. "According to my records, Jadzia suffered so much radiation exposure in the final struggle that she had only a few hours to live. Rather than stay aboard, she took a lifepod and created a diversion for the aliens who were attacking us. That's how the ship finally got away."

"Got away?" Sisko demanded in disbelief. "You mean some of the crew survived the battle we just saw?"

Bashir grimaced. "How do you think those medical logs got written up? I not only survived the battle, Captain, I appear to have lived for a considerable time afterward. There are several years' worth of logs here, if not more."

"Several *years?*" It was Dax's turn to sound incredulous. "You stayed on board the *Defiant* for several years after this battle, Julian? And no one came to rescue you?"

"No."

"That can't be true!" The *Defiant*'s captain vaulted from his chair, as if his churning restlessness couldn't be contained in one place any longer. "Even a totally disabled starship can emit an automatic distress call," he growled. "If no one from Starfleet was alive to respond to it, some other Federation ship should have. *Was our entire civilization destroyed?*"

"No," Hayman said soberly. "The reason's much simpler than that, and much worse. Come with me, and I'll show you."

Cold mist ghosted out at them when the fusion-bay doors opened, making Dax shiver and stop on the threshold. Beside her, she could see Sisko eye the interior with a mixture of foreboding and awe. This immense dark space held a special place in human history, Dax knew. It was the first place where interstellar fusion engines had been fired, the necessary step that eventually led to this solar system's entry into the federation of spacefaring races. She peered through the interior fog of subliming carbon dioxide and water droplets, but aside from a distant tangle of gantry lights, all she could see was the mist.

"Sorry about the condensate," Admiral Hayman said briskly. "We never bothered to seal off the walls, since we usually keep this bay at zero P and T." She palmed open a locker beside the ring doors and handed them belt jets, then launched herself into the mist-filled bay with the graceful arc of a diver. Sisko rolled into the hold with less grace but equal efficiency, followed by the slender sliver of movement that was Bashir. Dax took a deep breath and vaulted after them, feeling the familiar interior lurch of the symbiont in its pouch as their bodies adjusted to the lack of gravitational acceleration.

"This way." The delayed echo of Hayman's voice told Dax that the old fusion bay was widening as they moved farther into the mist, although she could no longer see its ice-carved sides. She fired her belt jets to follow the sound of the admiral's graveled voice, feeling the exposed freckles on her face and neck prickle with cold in the zero-centigrade air. Three silent shadows loomed in the fog ahead of her, backlit by the approaching gantry lights. She jetted into an athletic arc calculated to bring her up beside them.

"So, Admiral, what have you—"

Her voice broke off abruptly, when she saw what filled the space in front of her. The heat of the work lights had driven back the mist, making a halo of clear space around the dark object that was their focus. At first, all she saw was a huge lump of cometary ice, black-crusted over glacial blue gleaming. Then her eye caught a skeletal feathering of old metal buried in that ice, and followed it around an oddly familiar curve until it met another, more definite sweep of metal. Beyond that lay a stubby wing, gashed through with ice-filled fractures. She took in a deep, icy breath as the realization hit her.

"That's the *Defiant!*"

"Or what's left of her." Sisko's voice rang grim echoes off the distant walls of the hold. Now that she had recognized the ship's odd angle in the ice, Dax could see that he was right. The port nacelle was sheared off entirely, and a huge torpedo-impact crater had exploded into most of the starboard hull and decking. Phaser burns streaked the *Defiant*'s flanks, and odd unfamiliar gashes had sliced her to vacuum in several places.

She glanced across at Hayman. "Where was this found, Judith?"

"Right here in Earth's Oort cloud," the admiral said, without taking her eyes from the half-buried starship. "A mining expedition from the Pluto LaGrangian colonies, out prospecting for water-cored comets, found it two days ago after a trial phaser blast. They recognized the Starfleet markings and called us, but it was too fragile to free with phasers out there. We had to bring it in and let the cometary matrix melt around it."

"But if it was that fragile—" Dax frowned, her scientist's brain automatically calculating metal fatigue under deep-space conditions, while her emotions kept insisting that what she was seeing was impossible. "It must have been buried inside that comet for thousands of years!"

"Almost five millennia," Hayman agreed. "According to thermal spectroscopy of the ice around it, and radiometric dating of the—er—the organic contents of the ship."

"You mean, the bodies," Bashir said, breaking his stark silence at last.

"Yes." Hayman jetted toward the far side of the ice-sheathed ship, where a brighter arc of lights was trained on the *Defiant*'s main hatch. "There's a slight discrepancy between the individual radiocarbon ages of the two survivors, apparently as a result of—"

"—differential survival times." The doctor finished the sentence so decisively that Dax suspected he'd already known that from his medical logs. She glanced at him as they followed Hayman toward the ship, puzzled by the sudden urgency in his voice. "How much of a discrepancy in ages was there? More than a hundred years?"

"No, about half that." The admiral glanced over her shoulder, the quizzical look back in her eyes.

"Humans don't generally live long enough to survive each other by more than a hundred years, Doctor."

Dax heard the quick intake of Bashir's breath that told her he was startled. "Both bodies you found were human?"

"Yes." Hayman paused in front of the open hatch, blocking it with one long arm when Sisko would have jetted past her. "I'd better warn you that, aside from microsampling for radiocarbon dates, we've left the remains just as they were found in the medical bay. One was in stasis, but the other—wasn't."

"Understood." Sisko pushed past her into the dim hatchway, the cold control of his voice telling Dax how much he hated seeing the wreckage of the first ship he'd ever commanded. She let Bashir enter next, sensing the doctor's fierce impatience from the way his fingers had whitened around his tricorder. When she would have jetted after him, Hayman touched her shoulder and made her pause.

"I know your new host is a scientist, Dax. Does that mean you've already guessed what happened here?"

Dax gave the older woman a curious look. "It seems fairly self-evident, Admiral. In some future timeline, the *Defiant* is going to be destroyed in a battle so enormous that it will get thrown back in time and halfway across the galaxy. That's why no one could come to rescue Julian."

Hayman nodded, her voice deepening a little. "I

just want you to know before you go in—right now, Starfleet's highest priority is to avoid entering that timeline. At all costs." She gave Dax's shoulder a final squeeze, then released her. "Remember that."

"I will." Although she managed to keep her tone as level as always, somewhere inside Dax a tendril of doubt curled from symbiont to host. Curzon's stored memories told Jadzia that when he knew her, this silver-haired admiral had been one of Starfleet's most pragmatic and imperturbable starship captains. Any future that could put that kind of intensity into Hayman's voice wasn't one Dax wanted to think about.

Now she was going to see it.

Inside the *Defiant,* stasis generators made a trail of red lights up the main turbolift shaft, and Dax suspected the half-visible glimmer of their fields was all that kept its crumbling metal walls intact. It looked as though this part of the ship had suffered one of the hull breaches O'Brien had reported, or some even bigger explosion. The turbolift car was a collapsed cage of oxidized steel resin and ceramic planks. Dax eased herself into the open shaft above it, careful not to touch anything as she jetted upward.

"Captain?" she called up into the echoing darkness.

"On the bridge." Sisko's voice echoed oddly off the muffling silence of the stasis fields. Dax boosted herself to the top of the turbolift shaft and then angled her jets to push through the shattered lift doors. Heat lamps had been set up here to melt away the ice still engulfing the *Defiant*'s navigations and science stations. The powerful buzz of their filaments and the constant drip and sizzle of melting water filled the bridge with noise. Sisko stood alone in the midst of it, his face set in stony lines. She guessed that Bashir had headed immediately for the starship's tiny medical bay.

"It's hard to believe it's really five thousand years old," Dax said, hearing the catch in her own voice. The familiar black panels and data stations of the bridge had suffered less damage than the rest of the ship. Except for the sparkle of condensation off their dead screens, they looked as if all they needed was an influx of power to take up their jobs again. She glanced toward the ice-sheathed science station and shivered. Only two days ago, she'd helped O'Brien install a new sensor array in that console. She could still see the red gleam of its readouts beneath the ice—brand-new sensors that were now far older than her own internal symbiont.

Dax shook off the unreality of it and went to join Sisko at the command chair. Seeing the new sensor array had given her an idea. "Can you tell if there are any unfamiliar modifications on the bridge?" she asked the captain, knowing he had probably memorized the contours of his ship in a way she hadn't. "If so, they may indicate how far in our future this *Defiant* was when it got thrown back in time."

Sisko swung in a slow arc, his jets hissing. "I don't see anything unfamiliar. This could be the exact ship we left back at *Deep Space Nine*. If the Furies are going to invade, I'd guess it's going to be soon."

Hayman grunted from the doorway. "That's exactly the kind of information we needed you to give us, Captain. Now all we need to know is where and when they'll come, so we can be prepared to meet them."

"And this—this ghost from the future." Sisko reached out a hand as if to touch the *Defiant*'s dead helm, then dropped it again when it only stirred up the warning luminescence of a stasis field. "You think this can somehow help us find out—"

The chirp of his comm badge interrupted him. "Bashir to Sisko."

The captain frowned and palmed his badge. "Sisko here. Have you identified the bodies, Doctor?"

"Yes, sir." There was a decidedly odd note in Bashir's voice, Dax thought. Of course, it couldn't be easy examining your own corpse, or those of your closest friends. "The one in the ship's morgue sustained severe trauma before it hit stasis, but it's still recognizable as yours. There wasn't much left of the other, but based on preliminary genetic analysis of some bone fragments, I'll hazard a guess that it used to be me." Dax heard the sound of a slightly unsteady breath. "There's something else down here, Captain. Something I think you and—and Jadzia ought to see."

She exchanged speculative looks with Sisko. For all his youth, there wasn't much that could shatter Julian Bashir's composure when it came to medical matters. "We're on our way," the captain told him. "Sisko out."

Diving back into the shattered darkness of the main turbolift, with the strong lights of the bridge now behind her, Dax could see what she'd missed on the way up—the pale, distant quiver of emergency lights from the *Defiant*'s tiny sickbay on the next deck down. She frowned and followed Sisko down the clammy service corridor toward it. "Is the ship's original power still on down here?" she demanded incredulously.

From the darkness behind her, she could hear Hayman snort. "Thanks to the size of the warp core on this overpowered attack ship of yours, yes. With all the other systems shut down except for life-support, the power drain was reduced to a trickle. Our engineers think the lights and equipment in here could have run for another thousand years." She drifted to a gentle stop beside Dax and Sisko in the doorway of the tiny medical bay. "A tribute to Starfleet engineering. And to you too, apparently, Dr. Bashir."

The young physician looked up with a start from where he leaned over one of his two sickbay stasis units, as if he'd already forgotten that he'd summoned them here. The glow of thin green emergency lighting showed Dax the unaccustomed mixture of helplessness and self-reproach on his face.

"Right now, I'm not sure that's anything to be proud of," he said, sounding almost angry. His gesture indicated the stasis unit below him, which Dax now saw had been remodeled into an odd mass of pumps and power generators topped with a glass box. A fierce shiver of apprehension climbed up the freckles on her spine and made her head ache. "Why haven't you people done anything about this?"

Admiral Hayman's steady glance traveled from him to Dax, and then back again. "Because we were waiting for you."

That was all the confirmation Dax needed. She pushed past Sisko, and was startled to find herself dropped abruptly to the floor when the sickbay's artificial gravity caught her. Just a little under one Earth standard, she guessed from the feel of it—she felt oddly light and off-balance as she joined Bashir on the other side of that carefully remodeled medical station.

"Julian, is it . . . ?"

His clear brown eyes met hers across the misted top of the box. "I'm afraid so," he said softly, and moved his hand. Below where the warmth of his skin had penetrated the stasis-fogged glass, the mist had cleared a little. It was enough to show Dax what Bashir had already seen—the unmistakable gray-white mass of a naked Trill symbiont, immersed in brine that held a frozen glitter of bioelectric activity.

She had to take a deep breath before she located her voice, but this time her symbiont's long years of experience stood her in good stead. "Well," she said slowly, gazing down at the part of herself that was now immeasurably older. "Now I know why I'm here."

YR1,DY6,2340

Patient immobile + unresponsive. Limited contact + manipulation of subject due to fragile physical state and possible radiation damage, no invasive px/tx until vitals, Tokal-Benar's stabilize. Fluid isoboramine values <47%, biospectral scan=cortical activity < prev. observed norm, ion concentration still unstable. (see lab/chem results, atta) No waste products yet; adjusted nutrient mix +10% in hopes of improving uptake. Am beginning to fear I can't really keep it alive after all.

Staring down into the milky shadows of the suspension tank, Julian Bashir blinked away the image of those old medical records and trailed a hand across the invisible barrier separating the two realities. The stasis field pricked at his palm like a swarm of sleepy bees. "I guess I was wrong."

"Does that mean you don't think it's still alive?"

Bashir jerked his head up, embarrassment at being overheard smothering under a flush of guilt as soon as the meaning of Hayman's words sank in. He pulled his hand away from the forcefield, then ended up clenching it at his side when he could find nothing else to do with it. "No, I'm fairly certain it's still living." At least, that's what the readouts frozen beneath the stasis field's glow seemed to indicate. "It was alive when the field was activated five thousand years ago, at any rate. I can't tell anything else about its condition without examining it in real time." Although the thought of holding the orphaned symbiont in his hands made his throat hurt.

Across the table from him, Hayman folded her arms and frowned down at the shimmering box. The watery green of the emergency lights turned her eyes an emotionless bronze, and painted her hair with neon streaks where there should have been silver. "Assuming it's in fairly stable condition, what equipment would you need to transfer this symbiont into a Trill host?"

The question struck him like a blow to the stomach. "You can't be serious!" But he knew she was, knew it the very moment she asked. "Admiral, you can't just change Trill symbionts the way you would a pair of socks! There are enormous risks unless very specific compatibility requirements are met—"

"What rejection?" Hayman freed one hand to wave at Dax, standing silently beside her. "It's the same symbiont she has inside her right now!"

It occurred to Bashir, not for the first time, that he didn't like this woman very much. He couldn't imagine what Curzon Dax had ever seen in her. "It's a genetically identical symbiont that is *five thousand years* out of balance with Jadzia! For all we know, the physiological similarities between the two Daxes could make it even harder for Jadzia to adjust to the psychological differences." Dax herself had withdrawn from the discussion almost from the beginning. She'd turned her attention instead toward the naked symbiont in its stasis-blurred coffin, and Bashir wondered which of her many personalities was responsible for the eerie blend of affection and grief he could read in her expression. He wished he could make Hayman understand the implications of toying with a creature that was truly legion. "These are *lives* we're talking about, Admiral, not inconveniences. Any one of the three could die if we attempt what you're suggesting."

Hayman glared at him with that chill superiority Bashir had learned to recognize as a line officer's way of saying that doctors only earned their MDs because they hadn't the stomach for regular Starfleet. "If we don't find out who carved up the *Defiant* and pitched her back into prehistory," she told him coldly, "millions of people could die."

He clenched his jaw, but said nothing. *That's the difference between us,* he thought with sudden clarity. As regular military, Hayman had the luxury of viewing sentient lives in terms of numbers and abstractions—saving one million mattered more than saving one, and whoever ended the war with the most survivors won. As a doctor, he had only the patient, and even a million patients came down to a single patient, handled over and over again. No amount of arithmetic comparison could make him disregard that duty. And thank God for that.

Hayman made a little noise of annoyance at his silence, and shifted her weight to a more threatening stance. "Do I have to make this an order, Dr. Bashir?"

He lifted his chin defiantly. "As the senior medical officer present, sir, Starfleet regulations allow me to countermand any order you give that I feel is not in the best interests of my patient." He flicked a stiff nod at the stasis chamber. "This is one of those orders."

Surprise and anger flashed scarlet across her cheeks. For one certain, anguished moment, Bashir saw himself slammed into a Starfleet brig for insubordination while Hayman did whatever she damn well pleased with the symbiont. It wasn't how he wanted things to go, but it also wasn't the first time that a clear vision of the consequences came several seconds behind his words. He opened his mouth to recant them—at least in part—just as the admiral turned to scowl at Sisko. "Captain, would you like to speak with your doctor?"

The captain lifted his eyebrows in deceptively mild inquiry. "Why?" He moved a few steps away from the second examining bed, the one that held the delicate tumble of bones that Bashir had scrupulously not dealt with after identifying whose they were. "He seems to be doing just fine to me."

Hayman blew an exasperated breath, and her frustration froze into a cloud of vapor on the air. Like dragon's breath. "Do I have to remind you people that you were brought here so Starfleet could help you avert your own deaths?"

"Not if it means treating Jadzia or either of the Daxes as a sacrifice," Bashir insisted.

Dax stirred at the foot of the examining table. "May I say something?"

Bashir kept his eyes locked on Hayman's, refusing the admiral even that small retreat. "Please do."

"Julian, I appreciate your concern for my welfare, and for everything you must have gone through to keep the symbiont alive all this time . . ." Dax reached out to spread her cool hand over his, and Bashir realized with a start that he'd slipped his hand onto the stasis field again. "But I don't think this is really your decision to make."

He felt his heart seize into a fist. "Jadzia—"

"Dax." She joggled his wrist gently as though trying to gain his attention. "I'm *Dax,* Julian. *This*—" She patted his hand on the top of the tank, and he looked where she wanted despite himself. *"This* is Dax, too." The pale gray blur was nestled in its bed of liquid like a just-formed infant in its mother's womb. "I trust you enough to be certain you didn't do this as some sort of academic exercise. Preserving the symbiont must have been something you knew for a fact that I wanted—that *Dax* wanted. And the only reason I can think of that I'd be willing to live in a tank like this for so many hundreds of years is the chance to warn us about what happened—to prevent it in any way I can."

Sisko came across the room, stopping behind Dax as though wanting to take her by the shoulders even though he didn't reach out. "We don't know that for certain, old man. And if we lose both you *and* the symbionts testing out a theory . . ." His voice trailed off, and Bashir found he wasn't reassured to know that Sisko was just as afraid of failure as he was.

"We're only talking about a temporary exchange," Dax persisted. "Julian has obviously managed to re-create a symbiont breeding pool well enough to sustain my current symbiont for the hour or two we'll need. And even if we were transplanting a completely incompatible symbiont—" She truned to Bashir again, silently challenging him to say she was wrong. "—Jadzia wouldn't start showing signs of rejection for at least six hours. That should give us plenty of time."

But being correct about the time frame didn't mean she was correct about the procedure. "There's still the psychological aspect," he said softly. "We don't know what the isolation has done to the symbiont's mental stability." His hand stiffened unwillingly on the top of the tank. "Or what that might do to yours."

Dax caught up his gaze with hers, the barest hint of a shared secret coloring her smile as she took his arms to hold him square in front of her, like a mother reassuring her child. "I know for a fact that even six months of exposure to mental instability can't destroy a Trill with seven lifetimes of good foundation. Six hours with some other aspect of myself isn't going to unhinge me." She let her smile widen, and it did nothing to calm the churning in his stomach. "You'll see."

"If you're not willing to perform the procedure, Doctor, I'm sure there are other physicians aboard this starbase who will."

Anger flared in him as though Hayman had thrown gasoline across a spark. Dax's hands tightened on his elbows, startling him into silence as she whirled to snap, "Judith, don't! I won't have him blackmailed into doing this."

The admiral's eyes widened, more surprised than irritated by the outburst, but she crossed her arms without commenting. A more insecure gesture than before, Bashir noticed. He was secretly glad. He didn't like being the only one unsure of himself at a time like this.

"What if there were some other way?" he asked Dax. She opened her mouth to answer, and he pushed on quickly, "Symbionts can communicate with one another without sharing a host, can't they? When they're in the breeding pools back on Trill—when you're in the breeding pools with them?"

The thought had apparently never occurred to her. One elegant eyebrow lifted, and Dax's focus shifted to somewhere invisible while she considered. "It doesn't transfer all the symbiont's knowledge the way a joining does," she acknowledged after a moment. "But, yes, direct communication is possible."

A little pulse of hope pushed at his heart. "And in a true joining, Jadzia wouldn't retain any of the symbiont's memories, anyway, once the symbiont was removed."

Dax nodded thoughtfully. "That's true."

"So what harm is there in trying this first?"

"Trying what first?" Hayman's confidence must not have been too badly damaged, because the impatient edge to her voice returned easily enough. "What are you two talking about?"

Bashir looked over Dax's shoulder at the admiral, schooling the dislike from his voice in an effort to sound more professional. "When they aren't inside a host, Trill symbionts use electrochemical signals to communicate with one another through the liquid they live in. Even a hosted symbiont can make contact with the others, if its host is first submerged in the fluid pool." He glanced aside at the tank while his thoughts raced a dozen steps ahead. "If we can replicate the nutrient mixture that's been supporting the symbiont, and fill a large enough receptacle, I think the Daxes should be able to . . ." He hesitated slightly, then fell back on the easiest word. ". . . talk to each other without having to remove Jadzia's current symbiont."

Hayman chewed the inside of her lip. "We could question this unhosted symbiont that way? It could talk to us through Dax?"

"Through Jadzia," Bashir corrected automatically, then felt heat flash into his cheeks at Hayman's reproving scowl. "Yes, we could."

"Julian's right." Dax saved him from the rest of the admiral's disapproval. "I think this will work."

"And if it doesn't work?" Hayman fixed Bashir with a suspicious glare, as if expecting him to lie to her. "What are our chances of losing the symbiont?"

"I don't know," he admitted. He wished the truth weren't so unhelpful. "I don't know how fragile it is, how much radiation damage it may have sustained back then. It may not live beyond removal of the stasis field, and I don't know what effect physically moving it from one tank to another might have." He looked into Dax's eyes so that she could see he was being absolutely honest, as a doctor and as her friend. "I do know it will be less traumatic than trying to accomplish a joining under these conditions."

Dax nodded her understanding with a little smile, then squeezed his arms once before releasing him to fold her own hands behind her back. "I think this will be our best option."

"All right, then." Hayman flashed Bashir an appreciative grin, all his sins just that quickly forgiven now that she had what she wanted. Bashir wondered if that was supposed to make him feel as guilty as it did.

"Let's give this a try. Lieutenant"—she gathered both Dax and Sisko to her side with a wave of one hand—"you and the captain can tell me how much fluid and what size tank we'll need, then help me get it all down here. Doctor, wake up the symbiont." She leaned across the tank to clap him manfully on the shoulder, and Bashir found he didn't like the contact. "Looks like it's time to finish what you started."

Look for
Star Trek Deep Space Nine®
Invasion! Book Three
Time's Enemy
Wherever Paperback Books Are Sold
Coming mid-July from
Pocket Books

STAR TREK®
PHASE II
THE LOST SERIES

Judith and Garfield Reeves-Stevens

STAR TREK PHASE II: THE LOST SERIES is the story of the missing chapter in the STAR TREK saga. The series, set to start production in 1977, would have reunited all of the original cast except Leonard Nimoy. However, Paramount Pictures decided to shift gears to feature film production, shutting down the television series. Full of never-before-seen color artwork, storyboards, blueprints, technical information and photos, this book reveals the vision behind Gene Roddenberry's lost glimpse of the future.

POCKET
B O O K S

Coming in mid-August in Hardcover
from Pocket Books

1217

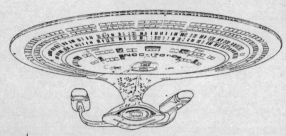